SICILIAN ESCAPE

Marianne Westlake arrives in Sicily desperate for a holiday after the end of her brief, unhappy marriage. She takes refuge with her brother's old friend, Gabe Alessandro, but the long-haired teenager she remembered is now a charming international businessman and their instant attraction threatens her fragile heart. Marianne's ex-husband, Gabe's would-be fiancée, and trouble in the Alessandro family hotel business challenge them to find the courage to move on from the past and make a bright future together.

ANGELA BRITNELL

SICILIAN ESCAPE

Complete and Unabridged

LINFORD
Leicester

First published in Great Britain in 2013

First Linford Edition
published 2014

A catalogue record for this book is available
from the British Library.

ISBN 978–1–4448–2152–9

Published by
F. A. Thorpe (Publishing)
Anstey, Leicestershire

Set by Words & Graphics Ltd.
Anstey, Leicestershire
Printed and bound in Great Britain by
T. J. International Ltd., Padstow, Cornwall

This book is printed on acid-free paper

1

The heat slammed into Marianne the instant she stepped off the plane in Catania. With a sigh she slung her overstuffed carry-on bag over her shoulder and strode across the shimmering hot tarmac into the crowded arrivals hall. Elbowing her way through noisy groups of passengers and welcoming families, her gaze flitted around, searching for a familiar face.

'Squib. Over here, Squib.'

The sound of her reviled childhood nickname made Marianne jerk around. A strikingly tall, ebony-haired man waved over the crowd and she automatically waved back. Starting to walk towards him, the closer she got the faster her heart raced. Surely the handsome broad-shouldered man with his designer suit, dark sunglasses, and charming smile couldn't be the scrawny, scruffy teenager she'd teased twelve years ago?

'Hey, Squib, come here.'

Suddenly she was grabbed by a pair of strong arms and hugged tight before being kissed European-style on both cheeks. Easing her away, he took off the glasses and fixed her with his dark, almost black eyes.

'What'd you do with Andy's little sister?' He trailed his fingers through her cropped-off light brown hair and smiled. 'No wild purple curls anymore? I'm disappointed.'

'I've grown up, like everyone, Gabe.' She heard the flatness in her voice and tried for a smile. 'You're not exactly like you were at nineteen either.'

'In a good way?'

His scrutiny made Marianne blush, completely disconcerted by this new version of her brother's old friend. 'I'll reserve judgement. Ask me again in a week.' She brushed off his slightly flirtatious enquiry.

'I'll hold you to that.' Taking hold of

her elbow, he steered her towards the baggage arrival area. 'I assume you checked a suitcase?'

She nodded and almost had to break into a run to keep up with his long legs. Bags were already going around the carousel but hers was easy to spot — there were never any other bright turquoise cases with hand-painted yellow daisies.

'It's that one.'

Gabe gave a wry smile but made no comment, only picked up her bag as though it weighed nothing at all.

'Let's head outside. I'll find you a shady spot where you can wait while I get the car.'

Feeling rather like an abandoned package, Marianne stood where she was told and watched him stride away. Before arriving she'd almost begun to believe Andy's theory that a change of scenery in the company of his old university friend and the rest of the Alessandro family would be a welcome change from her messy life. The trouble was, they'd all remembered Gabe as he was years ago, and the dramatic change added an extra layer of tension she could do without right now.

A loud screech of brakes next to Marianne startled her and she automatically jumped back away from the road. A flashy black open-topped sports car stopped right at her feet and Gabe leapt out. He came around to pick up her case, grinning like crazy and seemingly oblivious to everyone around them, staring with open curiosity. She could only suppose if you drove a car like that you got used to the effect it had wherever you went.

'Lucky you packed light, Squib. This little beauty isn't designed to hold a lot of luggage. Hop in and we'll get out of this mess.' He opened the passenger door and stood to one side while she lowered herself down into the soft leather seat.

As they pulled away from the terminal Marianne noticed several more people gawking at them.

'I could've brought the Fiat I use most of the time, but . . . '

'You wanted to show off.' A touch of added color tinged his sharp cheekbones but Gabe only shrugged and flashed a wide, white-toothed smile before turning back to concentrate on driving.

She slipped on her own sunglasses against the bright glare, the stunning azure sky a contrast to grey, rainy Plymouth. The glasses gave her the added bonus of being able to surreptitiously study Gabe better. He'd abandoned his suit jacket and tie and rolled up the sleeves of an immaculate white shirt. She wished it didn't draw her attention quite so much to his strong, tanned arms and his large hands resting easily on the steering wheel. Handsome men could cloud a woman's judgement and she had a brief six-month marriage and unfriendly divorce to attest to the fact. No way was she going there again in this lifetime; her heart wouldn't be

5

able to stand another bruising.

'We'll be out of the city soon and then head up the mountain. It'll take about an hour so you can either rest or take in the scenery.' He briefly glanced over at her, then away again. 'Feel free to talk if you want. It doesn't bother me either way.'

She didn't know how much her brother had told him, but if he thought she was telling him anything important he was wrong. Protecting her privacy and her heart were a priority. 'I believe I'll enjoy watching where we're going if you don't mind. Maybe you can tell me about some of the places as we're driving through.' She glanced around the car. 'That is, if we don't go so fast it's all a blur.'

Gabe's instant burst of warm laughter stirred a memory in Marianne of the gawky teenager making fun of himself when he'd got yet another English expression wrong.

'I can't do much with this baby on the local roads. They're far too narrow and with too many curves.' He grinned. 'Too many people and dogs in the way as well.'

'Why bother with it then?' She smoothed her hand over the glossy wood interior. Marianne didn't dare ask what it'd cost but suspected it'd make her jaw gape open if she found out.

'You should see how she goes on the racetrack — zero to a hundred clicks an hour in three point seven seconds. That's what you call an adrenaline rush,' he declared emphatically.

'It sounds scary to me, but I've never been one for extremes,' Marianne stated equally firmly right back at him.

'Are you sure? Apart from the always-changing crazy hairstyles, you had new piercings every time I visited — ears, nose, lips and goodness knows where else. Plus there were all the black clothes and creepy white make-up with black lips and eyes. You weren't exactly Miss Conventional, were you?' he teased.

Marianne gave a small shrug, not

sure she liked being reminded of her wild younger self. 'I was thirteen and I liked to be different. I've changed.' She turned her attention back to the road, hoping to make it clear this conversation wasn't going anywhere. He didn't reply but she noticed an amused curve to his mouth and guessed he was biting back laughter.

For the next half hour he negotiated the narrow winding roads in almost total silence. Occasionally he pointed out a spectacular view out over the Mediterranean, a particularly interesting old church in one of the small towns, or flamboyant brightly colored flowers tumbling down over the whitewashed walls of a house. She drank it all in, starting to relax and enjoy the experience.

Suddenly in front of them the snow-covered top of Mount Etna rose up into the crystal-clear blue sky. She gasped out loud.

'Spectacular, isn't it? When I'm away it's what I miss the most. It must be a woman, because its moods change with the wind; one day dark and brooding, then the next bathed in sunshine.'

Gabe's eloquence startled Marianne and for a second she didn't answer, confused at the change in his manner.

'I'd love to see it close up.'

'You shall. We'll take a trip to the top and you can look right down into the crater.' He gave a wicked grin. 'If it doesn't decide to erupt again.'

The blood drained from her face. 'Is that likely?'

His warm, firm hand covered hers, giving a gentle squeeze. 'Oh, *cara* — Marianna — it's been quiet for a while now, and the experts are good at predicting eruptions these days, so don't worry.' He gave her a kind smile. 'I'll keep you safe.'

Marianne wasn't certain of his ability to keep such a promise. Life recently had taught her to be wary. By simply getting off the plane she'd launched herself into a new environment, seemingly without a parachute, and the ground was getting closer by the second. 'Will your parents already be at the house when we arrive?' It wasn't easy to discern Gabe's reactions under the dark sunglasses but she noticed a tightening in his jaw.

'Didn't Andy tell you?'

What had her scheming big brother decided she didn't need to know?

'They're away on a cruise to celebrate my mother's birthday, which is why I'm here. I'm usually busy with our businesses in Milano and Firenze but there were some problems with our Etna hotel so Papa wanted me to sort things out.'

She wasn't staying in any house alone with Gabe Alessandro — old friend or not.

'Don't worry, Squib. Caterina and Antonio Palmetto stay in the house while I'm there. She cooks and cleans the house while he takes care of the garden and does anything else his wife tells him to.'

She didn't want him to be attracted

to her but wasn't sure how she felt about the fact he obviously found the idea amusing. 'By the way, I'd prefer you not to call me by that childish name. No one's called me that in years.'

'*Scuse*. Marianna. Is that better?'

'Almost, but there's no 'a' on the end of my name. It's an 'e.''

'That's the Italian pronunciation, *cara*.'

She gave up in the face of his polite stubbornness. They drove in silence until he turned onto a quiet side street. After passing a few solitary houses, a massive whitewashed house appeared in front of them, fronted by imposing black railings.

'This is my summer villa. Most of the houses up here are second homes for businessmen from the Catania area seeking to escape the heat with their families.' Gabe pressed a remote control and the large gates swung back.

'When you say it's yours, you mean it's the family home?'

'No, I meant what I said.' His dark eyes turned serious. 'I always do,

11

Marianna. It is wise for you to remember that.'

His words startled her.

'I needed my own place so had this built to my own design about four years ago. My parents live mostly in Napoli these days when they aren't travelling. I keep an upstairs wing of this house free for when they do visit.' He steered the car in around the paved circular driveway and stopped in front of the house.

'*Benvenuta*. Welcome.' Gabe turned off the engine, quickly got out and walked around to open her door.

'Thank you.' She stared around at the lush, colorful garden. 'This is incredible. Did you design it as well as the house?'

'I helped, with a lot of advice from experts.' He rubbed idly at his forehead. 'It's my retreat.'

'From what?' She bit her tongue and wished she hadn't asked. Gabe's personal life was nothing to do with her. 'I'm sorry, forget I asked.'

'Life, Marianna, just life.'

'It seems rather charmed to me,' she answered with a hint of bitterness.

'Everything is not what it seems. You should know that as well as anybody,' Gabe retorted.

How much had Andy told him? A hot blush crept up her face and she wished she'd stayed in London.

'Let's go inside.' His voice returned to its usual deep warmth. 'It will be all right, Marianna.'

What would? Staying here with him? Her messy life? Somehow she doubted both but dragged out a smile. 'Hopefully.'

The front door opened and a short, plump woman dressed all in black stepped out. She launched into a torrent of incomprehensible Italian aimed at Gabe and her tone of voice said she wasn't pleased. He replied and looked sheepish before turning back in her direction.

'Signora Palmetto says I'm an appalling host to leave you out here after such a brutal journey. She will tell my mother when she sees her and I deserve to be soundly beaten. I'm to bring you inside, let you freshen up and then she has cold drinks and snacks ready on the terrace.'

'That sounds wonderful.' Marianne smiled freely for the first time since arriving. 'I only hope your mother follows through.'

'She will, don't worry. The Palmettos have worked for my family for generations. If I annoy them in any way I'm in big trouble, trust me.' He laughed and turned back to the car and got out her bags before gesturing for her to lead the way.

Marianne walked into the expansive terracotta-tiled hall, gazed up at the wrought-iron spiral staircase leading to the upper storey, and around at the striking paintings decorating the walls and felt a brief frisson of excitement. The next few weeks would be a challenge, but maybe Andy had been right after all.

2

Marianne quietly took in the amazing view and sipped at her glass of light Prosecco wine. As the sun set myriads of lights from the tiny villages leading down the mountain to the sea twinkled and she let out a small sigh. She'd tried to do justice to the wonderful meal of antipasti, fettuccini Alfredo, veal scaloppini, and brandied peaches but it'd been a struggle.

'I won't be able to eat as much every night or I'll need to be rolled back on the plane when I go home.' She sensed rather than saw Gabe's smile, barely able to make out his face in the shadows.

'Don't worry. Caterina was out to impress you tonight.' He lowered his voice. 'Maybe I was too.'

'Why?'

'I suppose because you arrived with

15

certain ideas and I wanted to make it clear I'm not the same person anymore.'

'You mean the free-spirited young man with the flowing hair and plans to be the next Michelangelo? Is he buried under the designer suits and flashy car?' Marianne caught his quick intake of breath.

'He's long gone. I was young and foolish.'

She was almost afraid to speak in case she broke the fragile thread of understanding confidence. 'You were an incredibly talented painter.' Suddenly he pushed his chair back and walked over to the railing overlooking the hillside. She guessed he didn't want her to see his face. Perversely she stepped over to join him, but he kept his gaze fixed on the inky black sea.

'I had responsibilities and a duty to my family. You are very welcome here, but . . .'

'Under the condition I don't ask too much, right?'

He shrugged. 'I wouldn't exactly call it that.' Gabe turned and fixed her with his penetrating eyes. 'Andy warned me not to discuss your marriage so we both come with conditions.'

'Touché.' A wave of tiredness swept over her. 'I'm ready for bed if you'll excuse me.' His hand reached out to press her arm, stopping her from moving.

'*Scusa*, Marianna. That was inexcusable.'

'No, I let my tongue run away with me. Your choices are nothing to do with me.' Impulsively she reached up to touch his cheek. 'I genuinely am tired. Let's start afresh in the morning.' Gabe rested his large, strong hands on her shoulders and for a few brief seconds their eyes met and something strange and wonderful happened.

'Certainly. I'm going early over to the hotel.'

'To catch someone out?' she joked.

'Maybe, but Papa could be wrong.' Gabe frowned.

'Do you want to talk about it?'

17

Marianne asked cautiously. This was probably another item on the 'not for discussion' list.

'Not now. I haven't sorted it enough in my own mind yet, but I might ask your opinion later if that's all right?'

It came very close to an apology for his earlier behavior and she took it in the spirit with which it was offered. 'Of course.' She moved away and walked inside without looking back.

★　★　★

'Good morning, Signora Palmetto.' Marianne smiled at the older lady bustling around the kitchen.

'Caterina, you call me Caterina. You go out there and I bring you breakfast.' She waved her hand in the direction of the terrace. 'You like coffee?'

She'd actually prefer tea, but got the impression it wasn't a question. The mild air caressed her skin as she stepped outside. Marianne was drawn over by the railing again and took in the sight of the clear blue Mediterranean Sea spread out in front of her. Turning back around she glanced up at the mountain behind them, remembering Gabe's description of Etna as a changeable woman. Today she must be in a good mood, the snow-covered top disappearing up into sky the same color as the calm sea.

'There you go.' Caterina placed a tray of fresh fruit and pastries on the table along with a pot of coffee. 'Eat up. You're too skinny. I expect your mamma sent you here to get good food so Caterina will do her best.'

Was the woman a witch? It was the last thing her mother said before she left for the airport. The order was to stuff herself with pasta and not to work it all off with the long runs and bicycle rides she favored.

'Thank you, it looks delicious.' Marianne picked up a slice of melon. 'Is Gabe at work already?' The woman frowned hard — maybe she didn't understand English very well?

'Who is Gabe? I do not know anyone with that name.'

Maybe she was more formal with her employer. 'I mean Signor Alessandro.'

Caterina beamed, wrinkles creasing her dark leathery skin. 'Ah, Signor Dante. He go early, but he will be back for dinner. I take care of you.'

Being fussed over all day wasn't on Marianne's agenda, but she gave a polite smile and prepared to plot her escape. Idleness didn't suit her, giving her too much time to think. She'd investigate the nearest village today and would need to find things to fill the rest of the time until she returned home. The last thing she wanted was to get in Gabe's way. He was trying to pay back an old friend for long ago hospitality and Marianne didn't want him to regret his kind offer.

★ ★ ★

A screech of tires and then the front door slammed. Marianne could see into the hall from where she sat on the sofa, pretending to read her book. Caterina scuttled out from the kitchen and started jabbering away to Gabe. He answered and quickly extricated himself and walked straight into the living room.

'Ah, Marianna.' A quick grin lightened his serious face. 'See, I remembered. No more Squib.'

'Well done, you get ten bonus points. Should I return the favor and call you Dante? Caterina didn't understand who I was talking about when I called you Gabe.' A rush of heat colored his dark tanned skin.

'I don't mind. No one ever called me Gabe until Andy the first week we met at university. He laughed and said Dante was a girly name. If my mother's really cross it'll be the full Dante Gabriel Alessandro. My mother is an aficionado on Dante, so maybe she hoped I'd become a poet too.' He gave a wry grin.

'I'm not sure that's going to happen,

but I might be wrong,' she joked.

Gabe shook his head. 'No, you're absolutely right. I don't have a poetic bone in my body.'

She wasn't convinced but kept the thought to herself.

'I hear you've been into Pozzala this afternoon. Let me go up and change then we'll have a drink outside and you can tell me what you thought of our little town.' He picked up the suit coat he'd discarded on the way in and headed for the stairs.

Marianne put down the book, giving up on the attempt to read and waited.

'There, that's better.'

Gabe stood in front of her with his Armani suit, white shirt and polished black shoes replaced by linen shorts, an old red t-shirt, and leather sandals. Her heart raced and she couldn't help staring.

'I hope you don't mind but I've been stifled in those clothes all day.'

'Do I look like somebody bothered about designer fashion or the lack of it?'

22

Marianne gestured towards her own well-worn sleeveless cotton dress. 'You should be comfortable in your own home.'

He glanced down at her through his long, dark lashes. 'I'm not being critical but I remember you following the latest trends. What made you lose interest?'

She couldn't tell him the whole truth. 'Didn't Andy mention I'm a physical education teacher?'

Gabe shook his head. 'We haven't kept in touch. Men aren't great at keeping up friendships. We went our separate ways after graduation and didn't speak again until he phoned a couple of weeks ago.'

Marianne couldn't make herself talk about her marriage yet. 'I spend my days wearing sports gear and trainers and don't have much of a social life so there's rarely any reason to dress up.'

'You've nothing to apologize for.' He gave a shy smile and reached up to touch her cheek. 'Little Squib turned into a beautiful woman. I didn't expect that when I agreed to Andy's request.'

Her throat dried, preventing any attempt at an answer.

Gabe took a step back. 'Sorry. I'm out of line.'

Marianne still couldn't speak.

The buzzer in the hall rang several times and Gabe left her to go and answer it. He didn't sound too pleased at hearing who was at the gate. She peered out around and saw him open the door and walk outside to greet his guest.

Caterina bustled out from the kitchen, wiping her hands on her apron with disapproval written all over her stern face. Marianne's curiosity nearly exploded, wondering who'd caused this reaction. She didn't have to wait long to find out.

A strikingly beautiful woman with glossy, long dark hair strode in followed by Gabe. He smiled but Marianne sensed his uneasiness without understanding why.

'I'd like to introduce Signorina

Alexandra Rossini, an old friend of mine.'

The woman took a possessive hold of his arm. 'Now, now, Dante. I don't think this lady will believe that's true for a second.' Alexandra switched her attention to Marianne, piercing her with a sharp stare. 'Dante and I are, how you say, engaged to be married.'

'Oh.' She struggled to keep her composure. 'I see. Congratulations.'

'That's not strictly accurate, Alexandra,' Gabe protested.

'Not officially maybe, but it is understood.' Alexandra Rossini tried to sound conciliatory but the precise words belied his attempt to pacify her.

'This is not the time or place. We were about to have a drink on the terrace so would you care to join us?' Gabe slipped back into charming host mode.

The woman's dark eyes made Marianne shiver. 'I don't believe I will, Dante. It is a pleasure to meet you, Miss Westlake.' She fixed her attention firmly back on Gabe. 'You may pick me up at nine o'clock tomorrow night and book a table at Piccolini's.' Before he could answer she swept from the room, leaving behind a trail of expensive perfume and a silence throbbing with unanswered questions.

For a minute all Marianne and Gabe did was stare at each other.

3

'Go on outside and I'll fetch the wine,' Gabe stated in a voice which brooked no argument.

Marianne chose the same seat as last night and waited as he opened the bottle and poured two glasses of sparkling Prosecco. He drained his in one long swallow while she took one careful sip of her own and waited.

'Alex's family and mine have been friends for several generations. I grew up considering their house as a second home and Alex as the sister I didn't have.'

'She's a very beautiful woman.' Gabe nodded his agreement without looking too happy.

'Our families always encouraged our friendship, but . . . ' He stumbled over his words.

'Dante Gabriel Alessandro, that woman

does not think of you as a friend.' Marianne trotted out the names along with a mischievous grin. He didn't comment and took another swallow of wine before grabbing one of the delicious tomato bruschetta.

'No, and I'm to blame. About a year ago I was recovering here from a water-skiing accident and Alex caught me in a down moment. My actions led her to believe I saw a future for us. I've been too cowardly to tell her otherwise and that's not the action of a gentleman. I will sort it soon.'

'It's no business of mine. I'm only here as a guest for a couple of weeks. You can do whatever you like and it won't bother me in the least.' An unexpected sliver of jealousy shot through her. 'Let's change the subject.'

'Earlier tonight — what happened between us?' Gabe took her glass, put it down, and took hold of her hands. 'Something did, so don't pretend.'

She pulled away. 'I'm not pretending anything, but whatever it might have been I don't wish to take it any further.' Marianne took a deep breath. Some explanation was necessary but it'd be the bare minimum she could get away with. 'Andy told you I was briefly married. All I'll say is things went wrong and starting another relationship is nowhere on my radar and won't be for a very long time.'

'I'm sorry, but all men aren't the same you know.' Gabe's deep soft voice tugged at her heart. 'I'll say nothing more.'

'Thank you.'

'I'll tell Caterina we're ready for dinner.' Walking away he turned and gave the slightest of wicked smiles. 'Of course if you change your mind just let me know.'

He didn't wait for an answer, which was good because she didn't have one.

* * *

'Is it not to your taste?' Gabe pointed to the abandoned bolognese pasta on her plate.

'It's wonderful, but far too much.'

Tiny frown lines appeared between his dark eyes. 'Maybe I should stay silent but I remember you enjoying your food a lot more.'

Marianne forced out a laugh. 'In other words I was a chubby teenager. I try to eat healthy now and exercise a lot, that's all.'

He picked up her right hand, studying it intently. 'So fragile.'

Pulling away she took a long sip of her sparkling water. 'Don't be fooled. I'm very fit and strong. Run with me one day and I'll prove it.'

Gabe patted his flat stomach and chuckled. 'Are you saying I'm fat and couldn't keep up?'

She swallowed hard. 'You know that's not true, you vain man, so don't make me flatter you to appease your ego.' Keeping things light and friendly was important. 'Do you still cook?' Memories of a younger Gabe whisking up wonderful Italian specialties in their small kitchen at home flooded back.

Until then she'd only tasted her mother's spaghetti smothered with a ketchup-laden sauce not resembling anything ever served in Italy.

'Not often. I don't have the time or inclination.' Gabe fiddled with the stem of his wine glass.

'You don't cook for Alexandra?' His slightly twisted smile made her wish she hadn't asked.

'It'd be a waste of effort. Models aren't renowned for having healthy appetites and she eats less than you do.'

Marianne wanted to tell him she hadn't been this way until she met Robert Blackwell. 'Don't judge me, Gabe.' Something in her tone must've startled him because his eyes widened in surprise. 'I'm fine. Leave me alone.'

'I'm sorry. I promised Andy we'd be a haven for you and so far I've failed miserably. I'm off to Milano in the morning for a couple of days which will mean cancelling my dinner date with Alexandra.'

'What about the hotel problems here?'

'There's a meeting I need to attend in person so my father's concerns will have to be put on hold. A pilfering restaurant manager doesn't rank up there with finalizing a six-million-euro deal for a new hotel in London.'

'Can I do anything to help? Sitting around doing nothing doesn't suit me.' His softening glance told her he understood only too well.

'I'm not sure.' He shoved a hand through his thick, dark hair. 'This might not achieve anything, but I've an idea if you don't find it too mad.'

She grinned. 'You were never any crazier than me. Tell me what you're thinking.'

'You could check into the hotel as a guest, maybe claim you're looking for a quiet holiday while recovering from a recent illness.'

She encouraged him to carry on, already intrigued.

'All the staff speak English, some better than others, but the younger ones usually relish practicing on guests, so for a start encourage them.'

'What does your father suspect is going on?'

'The restaurant receipts are way down and don't match the amount of food bought by the kitchen. It may be credit card fraud of some sort. The chef could be in on it too. Perhaps they're selling on goods and pocketing the money?' Gabe's features darkened. 'We've also had several maids leave suddenly and I wonder if the manager might've, shall we say . . . ' He fiddled with the linen napkin, screwing it up before attempting to straighten it out again.

'Tried to get overly friendly?' She phrased it delicately as the subject obviously embarrassed him. 'I'd be happy to give it a try. Where is the hotel?'

'It's over in Trebellini, about an hour away.' He glanced around and lowered his voice. 'We'll have to make up a cover story for Caterina because her niece works there and I don't want her to warn Florenze.'

'How about saying I plan to rent a car and see something of the local area while you're gone?'

He smiled and picked up her hand. 'You're a genius.' Gabe idly played with her fingers. 'I'll get a car arranged for first thing tomorrow and give you directions. I suggest you turn up at the hotel asking for a room as if you spotted it driving along.'

'What if they're fully booked?'

A cynical smile creased his face. 'I wish. The Bella Rosa was my family's first hotel and used to be the premier hotel in the area, but since Enrico Galasso took over the place has gone downhill.'

'We've got a deal,' Marianne said with a lightness of heart she hadn't felt in a long time.

'Good. I'll tell Caterina we're ready to go straight on to dessert, or do you want a fish course as well?' He looked concerned.

'Not really, but won't she be

offended? It'll be an awful waste of food too.'

A grin lit up his handsome face. 'Don't worry. She has a couple of cats tucked away I'm not supposed to know about. I'm sure they'll profit from our dinner.'

'Why are they kept secret?'

He smirked. 'Because she doesn't think it proper, and I'm such an ogre she's afraid to ask for permission.'

'You're silly. She openly berated you the day I arrived. You don't frighten her one bit and rightly so.'

'I'll have you know top business executives tremble when I turn up for negotiations,' Gabe protested.

'That's as may be, but you don't scare Caterina in the least; or me for that matter. You might look imposing but I'm pretty certain you're a big softie underneath.'

Gabe threw up his hands in surrender. 'I give up. You women are all the same. Why women claim to want equality is beyond me — you've been superior for thousands of years, since caveman days.'

'True, and I'm pleased to hear one of your gender admit it for once.'

'I'll rustle up dessert and coffee if that suits you?' He swooped into a low bow and she agreed, although the idea of eating anything else turned her stomach. Of course the minute Gabe tempted her with a mouthful of creamy zabaglione she changed her mind. Maybe it was better he was leaving tomorrow. Marianne wished she was more certain. She didn't want to miss him.

4

She'd blithely assured Gabe driving here wasn't a problem, so thank goodness he couldn't see her mess up the directions for at least the third time. At last she spotted the red and white awning he'd told her to look out for, shading the front of the Hotel Bella Rosa. Marianne stopped the car on the street and got out, taking time to notice how shabby the building looked, the hotel front door sorely in need of a fresh coat of paint. The minute she stepped inside the dark, cool lobby a short, neatly dressed man came out from behind the reception desk.

'Enrico Galasso at your service. I have the finest room available for the Signorina.' He slyly eyed her up and down. 'It is Signorina?'

Maybe she should claim to be married? Marianne put on her sharpest teacher's voice. 'Nothing too expensive. A simple room will suit me quite well for a few days.'

He bowed slightly. 'Dinner starts at eight if you wish to eat with us?'

'I believe I will. I'm tired and will be happy to stay in this evening.'

'I'll show you to your room.'

'Please don't trouble yourself.' She worked on sounding very decisive.

'Whatever you prefer,' he conceded, handing over a heavy bronze key. 'Room number twelve on the second floor.' Galasso pointed towards the stairs. 'There's a lift over in the corner if you prefer.'

Marianne glanced at the rickety-looking iron cage and chose to give it a miss, picked up her small bag and prepared to start her spying mission.

* * *

She purposely chose a high-necked, plain blue dress for dinner, and wore no makeup to look more tired and back up her story of recovering from a recent illness. Marianne pulled at the loose folds of material around her waist, unable to remember it being this big. She took out her mobile and texted Gabe. They'd agreed phoning from the hotel was too risky in case she was overheard so she'd send text messages, then try to ring when she was out. He immediately replied. 'Well done. Take care.' Her throat tightened at his obvious concern. She'd head downstairs and get to work.

'Signorina Westlake. My name is Florenze.' The shy, dark-eyed waitress showed her to a table by the window, perfect for watching out over the tiny town square. It was easy to ask for help with the menu and the girl visibly enjoyed showing off her more than passable English.

Marianne picked at a plate of indifferent pasta before managing about half of a small, tough veal chop. Even if the chef wasn't a crook she'd definitely recommend Gabe replace him. 'Have you worked here long?' she asked as the waitress came to clear her table.

'Two summers, Signorina.'

'Do you enjoy it?' A brief shadow flitted across the girl's face before she nodded. Marianne needed to back off for now and try again later. 'I believe I'll take a short walk. Could you bring me the bill please?'

Florenze glanced nervously around. 'I can put it on your hotel bill to settle when you leave.'

'No, thank you, I'd rather pay as I go.'

'Are you sure?'

The waitress's frown made Marianne wonder. Could the girl be trying to help her out or was she reading too much into everything? 'Yes I am,' she stated firmly and took out her purse while the girl disappeared back into the kitchen. Gabe had asked her to pay with cash today and with a credit card tomorrow. She purposely didn't study the bill too hard when it arrived, merely added a tip and handed over the money.

It was a relief to get back outside, but in case someone was watching she walked slowly by the nearby shops until she turned the corner into the next street and was out of sight. Marianne picked up her normal pace and strode along briskly, happy to feel a touch of her usual energy return. She made her way to the far end of the square and found a gelato shop busy with late-night customers. It was difficult to decide, but in the end pistachio won out and she took it back outside. Marianne ate all of the delicious, creamy treat then sat back and took out her dinner bill to examine.

She smiled at how stupid they were adding in a salad and glass of wine she hadn't ordered. Marianne tried to give Florenze the benefit of the doubt but it wasn't easy. She took out her phone and punched in Gabe's number.

'Ah, *cara* Marianna. How's my beautiful lady tonight?'

His deep voice resonated strongly even from hundreds of miles away. 'Are you drunk, Dante Gabriel Alessandro?'

'Only at hearing from you.'

She heard the teasing lilt to his words and determined not to give him any leeway. 'Stop your nonsense and listen to me.'

'Yes, Signorina.'

She imagined him dramatically closing his lips and forced a laugh back down. 'Your employees are not very intelligent and obviously rely on catching out ignorant tourists who don't know any better.' Marianne gave him a rundown on exactly what'd transpired. 'I may be wrong but I don't think Florenze's willingly in on this. I'll try to talk to her some more in the morning if I get the chance.'

'You're doing a great job, although I'm disappointed because I'd hoped my father was wrong.' He hesitated and she wanted to tell him to stop there. 'Do you miss me?'

'Why would I?'

'I don't know, you tell me.'

'Don't play games with me, Gabe.

Save that for Alexandra.'

'That's unkind, Marianna.'

'I've had to be recently.'

'Was that a warning?' he murmured.

'Take it how you want.' It wasn't a gracious way to speak but she had to protect herself.

'I refuse to say good night in anger, Marianna. I'm sorry. I spoke out of turn again.'

His obvious sincerity flooded her with guilt for her bad manners. 'I'm sorry too, Gabe, but you . . . ' She floundered, unable to put into words how he made her feel.

'Forget it, Squib.'

The old endearment made her smile again. 'Tell me about your day instead.' She relaxed and listened as he related amusing stories about his business dealings. Gabe made her laugh out loud with his description of one particular manager, with his overly pointed shoes and combed-over hair.

'I'd better let you go; it's late. We'll talk tomorrow,' Gabe said after a while.

'Good night.'

'Make sure you lock your door. If that man says anything . . . '

'I can handle myself. He'll discover the power of a well-aimed karate kick if he tries anything silly.'

'That's my girl.'

A strange silence hung between them for a moment. Marianne quietly said goodbye without commenting on his last statement.

★ ★ ★

Over an uninteresting breakfast of stale bread rolls and harsh coffee Marianne planned out her day. She'd start with a stroll around the town before returning to the hotel for lunch, then make it clear she was weary and retire to her room for an afternoon siesta. Maybe she'd take a short drive out later in the day before coming back for dinner. Her appetite must be improving because she found the prospect of more hotel meals distinctly unappealing.

Thankfully Signor Galasso was talking on the phone as she went back through the lobby which allowed her to sneak by and head back upstairs. Her bedroom door was open and the maid's cleaning cart stood outside.

Marianne breezed inside. 'Good morning, Florenze. Don't let me stop you. I'll sit on the balcony out of your way and read for a while.'

'Oh, Signorina, I am supposed to leave and come back later if someone wants their room.'

'I won't tell if you don't,' Marianne answered lightly, wanting the girl to know she could be trusted. She picked up her paperback from beside the bed and opened back the doors to the tiny balcony. She made herself comfortable on one of the wrought-iron chairs and kept an eye on Florenze as she worked. Thinking of her teenage pupils helped her decide how to get the maid talking. Flattery often worked, picking up on something they were good at. 'Where did you learn your excellent English?'

45

Florenze turned around and beamed. 'It's not so good really,' she said, modestly lowering her gaze to the tiled floor. 'We all learn at school.'

'You must have done more than that,' Marianne probed.

'I go to the local college two evenings a week.' She seemed unsure whether to continue, glancing back over her shoulder at the door. 'I want to work in Rome in big hotel.' Florenze blushed. 'I would like to be manager one day.'

'You're smart. You'll do it,' Marianne said in encouragement but the girl shook her head.

'My family does not wish me to go. They say Rome is bad for young woman. Also they . . . '

'Yes, is there something else?' Marianne held her breath.

'They want me to marry.'

Now she must be careful. 'Marriage is a good thing but maybe you are not ready yet?' Marianne inched her way towards finding the right thing to say

46

next. 'Is there a man your family favors?'

Florenze's smile faded and she picked up the duster she'd abandoned a few minutes earlier. 'It is not right to talk about my family business to strangers.'

'I'm sorry. I didn't mean to pry.' She wanted to add one more thing but phrasing it was delicate. 'If you'd like to talk again I'll be here all afternoon. We could have a drink together or maybe some ice cream. I'd enjoy your company.'

'I will be busy.' Florenze turned abruptly away and started to dust rather vigorously. Marianne nodded and picked up her book again while her mind raced like a caged hamster, busily planning her next move.

5

What a long, frustrating day it'd been so far. Marianne lay in the old-fashioned, claw-footed bath and stared up at the ornate plaster ceiling. After the episode with Florenze she'd itched to put on her running shoes and pound the roads around Trebellini but it didn't fit with the pale, lethargic image she was cultivating. Dutifully she'd taken a sedate walk around the village and sat idly at one of the cafés, making a tall glass of orange juice last as long as possible. Then it'd been time for another plodding lunch before another siesta. It was amazing she wasn't screaming with boredom. So much for intrigue. Maybe being a spy wasn't so fascinating after all.

Marianne played with the perfumed bubbles and considered ringing Gabe, but needing to hear his voice wasn't sufficient justification for breaking their agreement. She gave up on enjoying her bath and got out to dry off. For now she slipped on a short pink cotton dress and went out onto the balcony to enjoy the warm early evening air.

A light tap on the door disturbed her musings and she went to answer, hoping it might be Florenze. Enrico Galasso almost pushed his way in holding a bottle of wine and two glasses. He gave her a wide, unnerving smile and Marianne wished she'd chosen to wear a full suit of armor instead of the thin dress.

'*Buona sera*, Signorina. I thought you might enjoy an aperitif before dinner.'

She struggled to sound unconcerned. 'I don't believe I will, but thank you.'

Galasso ignored her and put down the items he carried on a nearby table. 'That is not very friendly, Signorina. I like to get to know my guests.'

Marianne put a hand to her head and prepared to convince him she wasn't well. 'I'm sorry but I've been very ill recently and came here for peace and quiet to recover.' She glanced over at the wine. 'I'm afraid the medicine I'm taking means I have to be careful and I'd rather have a glass of wine with my meal later.'

He gave a polite nod. 'Of course, but surely a little company would cheer you?'

The mobile phone lying on her bedside table started to buzz and she mentally gave thanks. 'Excuse me, I'm expecting a call.' The manager made no move to leave so she ignored him and answered, almost sagging with relief to hear Gabe's cheerful voice.

'I'm sorry to call, but I needed to hear your voice. How're you doing tonight?'

'Wonderful, darling. Missing you of course.'

'Really? Are you sure everything's all right?' She heard the wheels turn in his head. 'Is someone with you?'

'Yes, sweetheart. Hang on a minute.' Marianne gave the manager an apologetic shrug. 'I'm sorry but it's my boyfriend, do you mind?' Her lie gave him no alternative but to pick up his wine bottle and glasses and leave. She locked the door after him and sat down on the bed.

'What on earth was that about, and since when have I been promoted to boyfriend?' He sounded amused.

'That was your illustrious hotel manager offering to keep a lonely tourist company.' Gabe instantly let out what she guessed were a string of curses. 'I'm fine, honestly.'

'I shouldn't have put you in this situation. I can't imagine what I was thinking. My mama will beat me from one side of the island to the other if she ever finds out, and rightly so. You must leave immediately.'

She bridled at his authoritative tone. 'Don't be ridiculous. I'm a grown woman and he's nothing more than an annoying flirt.'

'I'm not convinced.'

'Well I am, so let's change the subject. Tell me about your day.' She lay back on the pillows and smiled as he launched into everything that'd happened since they spoke the night before.

'What're your plans for the evening?' he asked.

'I'm braving another dinner here tonight as instructed although I need to change first.'

'Why?'

'I need something more covered to face our friend again.'

'What color is the one you're wearing?'

'Um, pale pink, why?'

'Just imagining. Pretty.'

'Go and charm someone else or call Alexandra, she'll be pleased to hear from you I'm sure.'

His laugh rumbled down the phone. 'Very unkind, Marianna. I've just ordered room service and plan to watch the football on TV. Is that acceptable?'

'It doesn't bother me what you do. Why should it?'

'Maybe I want it to,' he whispered.

She sucked in a deep breath before answering. 'Then you shouldn't. I'm going now and I'll call later with an update.' They agreed and she quickly hung up.

So much for a peaceful, relaxing holiday. She'd sort out her brother when she got home.

* * *

Marianne examined the lumpy mass of pasta smothered in a thin cream sauce and wondered how little she could eat without arousing suspicion. Florenze was serving and kept looking as if she wanted to say something, but restricted herself to asking whether Marianne wanted more water or by tidying away imaginary crumbs off the table.

'Have you finished, Signorina?' Florenze gestured towards the almost full plate.

'Yes, thank you. I'm not very hungry tonight. Could you please bring me the bill? I don't want to hold you all up.'

Again there was that same frown. 'I'd like to put it on my credit card tonight, if that's all right?' She didn't imagine the rush of color creeping up the waitress's neck.

'I don't know if the machine is working, let me check.' Florenze almost ran back to the kitchen and as she went through the door Marianne noticed the manager grab her arm and pull her inside. She forced herself to stay seated.

'Any good?' She smiled at the girl, certain now that if Florenze was in on the fraud it wasn't by choice.

'Yes. I will take the card and put through the machine then bring right back, okay?'

'Of course.' Marianne handed it over and went back to finishing her glass of Chianti, purposely not watching the waitress.

'There you are.'

Florenze returned the card and gave her the bill to sign. Marianne added a generous tip and took her copy, tucking it away carefully into her purse. 'Thank you. I believe I'll take a short walk and maybe get an espresso at the café over by the church.' She couldn't spell it out any clearer.

Ducking out of the front door she ambled slowly down through the square. She loved being part of the life going on around her. Families walked along showing off their beautifully dressed children, and the local teenagers strutted and preened waiting to be noticed. Marianne chose a table where she had a good view of the mountain and noticed the top was hidden in a mass of dark clouds tonight. Gabe would say Etna was in a changeable mood and could go either way — to happiness or bad temper.

'Did you mean what you said yesterday, Signorina Westlake?' Florenze suddenly appeared by the table, frowning and sneaking anxious looks round. 'About the fact you wouldn't tell about anything I share with you?'

Tricky. If she promised it meant she couldn't tell Gabe, and he'd sent her here for a reason. On the other hand this girl plainly needed someone to talk to and felt she could trust her. Marianne swallowed her misgivings and nodded, unsure what she'd do if it was something Gabe needed to know. She gestured to Florenze to join her and waited.

'You asked about the man my family want me to marry. It is Philippe Galasso, the hotel cook. He is Signor Galasso's eldest son. My father believes Philippe's a good man, but he isn't.'

'Obviously I don't know him, but . . . he's a terrible cook and his father makes me very uneasy.' She smiled a little, wanting to say a lot more, but held her tongue.

'The food is awful isn't it, Signorina? I won't eat anything he cooks. Even the local dogs won't eat the leftovers we throw out, and Sicilian dogs usually eat anything.' She giggled.

'It's pretty bad. You don't have many customers and I seem to be the only hotel guest at the moment. How on earth do you stay open?'

Florenze looked distinctly awkward now. 'I do not think the owners realize how bad things are.'

'Surely they check the accounts? The numbers can't look very healthy.' The girl didn't quite meet her gaze and another suspicion slipped into place regarding the possibility of duplicate sets of accounts. Things might be even worse than Gabe realized and she didn't look forward to being the one passing on that nugget of information.

'I do not know Signorina, but Philippe is pressing me to become engaged and so is my father. I'm not sure how much longer I can say no without giving a reason.'

Marianne couldn't sit back and watch this charming girl driven into a loveless marriage. 'It's not my business but I'd advise you to be honest with your father. Tell him why you can't marry Philippe and I'm sure he won't force you. He can't, Florenze — you are a grown woman and have the right to choose your own husband.' The girl's response was a heartbreaking sigh.

'You are right, I know, but it is not that easy.' She swallowed hard. 'My father owes Signor Galasso money. A few years ago he was injured and couldn't work for many months so he borrowed money from Enrico Galasso, and now the interest keeps getting higher and he never gets caught up. If I marry Philippe the debt will go away.'

This got worse and more tangled by the minute. 'That is difficult, but if you could get work in a big hotel in Rome you would surely earn enough to pay it off?'

'I need to do more English classes and my father say he will not pay for any more.'

Marianne reined back the urge to offer the girl money on Gabe's behalf. He'd willingly pay for information about the fraud going on, but the second she suggested such a thing this tentative friendship would be over. Was she any better than the Galassos in using this kind girl for her own purposes? It'd sounded a straightforward task, but now she wished she'd never heard of the Hotel Bella Rosa or Gabe Alessandro's problems. She had her own money but this proud young woman wouldn't accept money from a virtual stranger. 'I'm so sorry. I wish I had an easy answer. Maybe if it continues to do so badly the hotel will close and your father won't be so keen on your marriage if Philippe is out of work?'

The girl smacked her hand hard on the table, making the glasses shake. 'Do not wish that for me. My family needs the money I bring home. That would make everything worse.'

'That was a stupid thing to say. I'm thoughtless.'

Florenze gave a small smile and patted Marianne's hand. 'No, you did not mean it in a bad way. I know you try to help.'

That was questionable. If she succeeded in what she'd come here to do the waitress would either be out of work, in trouble with the law, or both. Marianne had to smile and agree or tell the truth.

'I need to go home or my papa will worry. Will you stay here again tomorrow?' Florenze asked as she stood up.

'I'm not sure but I'll see you at breakfast anyway.'

'Thank you for trying to help. Good night.'

Marianne watched her go and tears pricked at her eyes. Her hands trembled as she tried to call Gabe on her mobile, making several mistakes before she got the numbers right on the fourth attempt.

'*Buona sera*, how's my favorite English lady tonight?'

'Awful. I shouldn't have agreed to do this.' She cut off his attempt to answer and poured out the whole story of her day, her throat catching when she told him about Signor Galasso's hold over Florenze's family.

'I'm so sorry for dragging you into

my concerns. I'll be home late tomorrow. We'll check your credit card statement online then and if there's anything else to do I'll take it from there.'

'What about Florenze?' All she could think of was the girl's innate sadness.

Gabe hesitated. 'I feel for her too, but at the moment I can't see what we can do to help.'

'So you'll just throw her to the wolves?' Marianne snapped, annoyed when he dared to laugh.

'Oh, Marianna, and you say we Italians are overly dramatic. No one is kidnapping her and forcing her to marry Philippe. This is not the middle ages you know.'

'You of all people should understand about family duty.'

'What exactly do you mean?' Gabe's voice turned icy.

She'd started so didn't have much choice but to carry on. 'Running a hotel empire wasn't what the young man I knew planned for his life.'

'That's in the past, Squib. I was ignorant and foolish.'

'Maybe Florenze's family would say the same? Who are we to judge?'

'I'm not discussing this any more over the phone. We'll talk when I get home,' he stated very decisively. 'Go and get some sleep and make sure to lock the bedroom door. I will see you tomorrow.'

She forced out a civil goodnight. The slower the time passed until their unwanted talk the better.

6

The black gates swung open and Marianne drove carefully inside before parking over by the side of the house out of the way. The sight of Caterina, solid and welcoming, smiling from the open front door, lifted her spirits and pushed thoughts of Gabe's return to the back of her mind. She willingly allowed Antonio to carry her bags up to her room and Caterina to produce a tray of coffee and pastries. After the dreadful food she'd endured the last couple of days she ate heartily, laughing to herself as she picked up a third cake. What a pity Gabe wasn't here to see her.

'Signor Dante wants dinner served late so he'll be here to eat with you. You should rest now. If you get hungry come to the kitchen and I can find you something.'

'I'm sure you will.' Marianne didn't bother arguing and obediently headed up the spiral staircase. She didn't expect to sleep but the stress of the last couple of days must've got to her because the next thing she knew it was seven o'clock. After a quick bath she dressed and put on a little light makeup before heading downstairs.

'I was hoping for the pink dress.' Gabe's dark eyes shone as he turned around from where he'd been looking out over the terrace.

'It needs to be washed so you'll have to make do with this instead.' She waved a hand down over her knee-length dark blue linen shift.

'Ah well, such is life.' He smiled and stepped over to the table. 'Wine?'

'Yes, please.'

He poured two glasses of her new favorite, the light sparkling Prosecco wine which would always be synonymous with Sicily and Gabe.

'Here's to enjoying a wonderful meal together and no serious talk until afterwards.' He raised his glass in a toast and Marianne responded, happy to prolong the difficult conversation to come.

Over dinner they talked, discussing everything from the delicious food, the Italian football team's recent loss and on to some of his favorite plants that'd come into flower while he was gone.

'Did you enjoy everything tonight?' He gestured towards the remains of the chocolate tart left on the table between them.

'Yes, it was divine. That's the most I've eaten in a long time.'

'Good.' Gabe studied her thoughtfully. 'I'm guessing it's better than the last couple of days?'

She'd been lulled into briefly forgetting and suddenly all pleasure disappeared from the evening. Gabe leaned across the table to cover her hand with his own, and the comforting squeeze he gave her fingers almost brought tears spilling from her eyes.

'I'm sorry. We can wait if you prefer.'

Marianne shook her head. 'No, let's get it over with.'

'Please don't take all this personally. I'm not criticizing you for anything when you've tried so hard to help me. I'm not a brute.'

His softly pleading voice startled her. Did he think it was how she saw him? Maybe she'd unintentionally given that impression on the phone last night? 'Oh, Gabe.' Impulsively she touched his cheek, feeling the slight roughness under her fingers.

'Sorry. I was too tired to shave.'

'That's all right. Let's start again.' She dropped her hand back to the table and picked up her espresso to take a steadying sip.

Gabe pushed back his chair. 'I'll bring down my laptop and we'll check your credit card first.'

It didn't take long for him to return and start to tap rapidly on the keys. 'Not very original.' He frowned. 'That's an old trick — increasing the size of the tip after the customer's signed the slip.

Very few people check their monthly statement closely enough to notice a few euros here or there.' Gabe sighed and shoved his fingers through his hair in frustration.

She ran through everything that'd happened because she hadn't been able to go into every detail on the phone. 'It's not good is it?' she asked, already knowing the answer.

'No, Marianna, it's not, and I suspect there's a lot more going on too. The supplies we've paid for don't match with the quantity of food sold in the restaurant. I'm guessing they're selling it on to other businesses and pocketing the money.' He hesitated then asked in a quiet voice, 'What's your opinion of Florenze now from the benefit of a little distance?'

Her instinct was to defend the girl but Marianne forced herself to be sensible. 'She's a good young woman, but I think she's been drawn into something she doesn't approve of and for a multitude of reasons couldn't say no.'

'Thank you,' Gabe murmured.

'What for?'

'Being honest. I really appreciate that. I don't want to get her into trouble — for a start I might lose Caterina and my stomach wouldn't be happy about that.' Gabe's attempt at humor faded and his face settled into serious lines. 'I owe it to my father to sort this out and I'm afraid she might be a casualty.'

Marianne nodded sadly. 'I realize that, and it saddens me.'

'Do you have any ideas, maybe something I haven't thought of?'

She straightened her shoulders and met his gaze straight on. 'I could get her alone and tell her the full story of why I was there and what I discovered. Then I'd give her the opportunity to share what she knows in return for leniency from you.'

Gabe shook his head in a very determined way. 'No, I can't let you do that. She'll turn on you and I should be the one bearing the brunt of her anger.'

'Now who's not being sensible? As if

she'll tell you anything. You'll frighten her into doing something stupid like running away.'

'Surely you don't think that's likely?'

Marianne shrugged. 'I don't know her well but she made it clear her family is very important to her and if this all comes out they'll be humiliated. We can't be responsible for that.'

'You're right.' He flashed a quirky smile in her direction. 'I hate to admit it of course, being a normal stubborn man.'

She gave in and smiled right back. 'I can't argue with that statement.'

'Let's think it over and decide after the weekend.' He looked thoughtful. 'You know what we need?' He didn't wait for an answer. 'How about a couple of days of fun and relaxation?'

Marianne sensed Gabe's definition of fun might be dangerous. 'What exactly do you have in mind?'

'Don't look so scared.' He grinned broadly. 'I promise I'll behave.'

'What are you thinking of?'

'Do you enjoy water sports?'

'I've done a little windsurfing and sailing and plenty of canoeing, but haven't had the opportunity to try anything else.'

'Good. I haven't taken any time off recently so I'll use you as an excuse.'

Marianne laughed. 'Please feel free.' She needed to say what was on her mind even if it annoyed him. 'Won't Alexandra mind?'

'I don't have to ask her permission, I thought I'd made that clear. Excuse me a moment while I make a call.' Gabe got out his phone and started talking in rapid Italian. Finally he smiled and set his mobile back down on the table. 'That's settled. My aunt and uncle have a beautiful place in Taormina and they'll be pleased to have us visit.'

'Didn't they mind you inviting yourself?'

Gabe chuckled. 'Not in the least. Why would they? They're always on at me to come and I'm rarely free. We'll leave tomorrow morning and be back on Sunday.' His gaze rested on her, sending a rush of heat to Marianne's cheeks. 'I assume you've brought swimsuits with you?'

'I've got one.'

'We'll pick you up a couple more; Taormina has many great shops. In fact I might never get you away from there and down to the beach,' he teased.

She burst out laughing. 'I'm no shopping fiend as you'll discover. If I find what I want in the first shop that will be it.'

'We'll see. You are still a woman when all's said and done,' he said with a smirk.

'Chauvinist.'

'Just stating facts, my Marianna.'

Before she could make any comment on his possessive words a series of loud explosions jolted her from her seat. 'What on earth is that?'

'Fireworks, what did you think it was?' he asked, obviously unconcerned.

'I don't know. Is there a special reason why tonight in particular?'

'No doubt it's one of the myriad of saints' days. Caterina would be able to tell us because she knows them all off by heart. All the villages have their patron saint so they celebrate their particular day, plus there're so many other holidays that warrant fireworks.' He stood and offered her his hand. 'Come over here and we'll watch together.'

Marianne couldn't resist and placed her right hand in his. He steered her in front of him and slid his arms around her waist, pulling her gently back against his warm body.

'It's coming from around Nicolosi somewhere,' Gabe murmured softly against her hair.

'Right.' She struggled to sound normal.

'Marianna.' Unexpectedly he swung her back around and a sudden burst of golden stars in the sky lit up his dark, handsome face. '*Sei cosi bella*, you're so beautiful, you're driving me crazy.'

'Signor Dante, you have a phone

call,' Caterina interrupted from the doorway into the house and they moved apart.

'Who is it?' he snapped, clearly not appreciating the interruption.

'It is your mamma calling from the ship. She tell me to hurry you, it is expensive.'

'Excuse me, Marianna.' He gave a small bow and strode off inside.

She met the older woman's curious stare. 'I hope nothing is wrong.' Caterina didn't answer, merely shook her head before going back into the villa.

A few minutes later Gabe returned, his eyes dark with worry. She held her breath and waited for him to speak.

7

'It's my father. The idiotic man tried windsurfing yesterday off Crete and broke his leg. He insisted on being flown back to the hospital in Naples but Mamma says not to go there. He's having surgery to set it this morning, and should be allowed home either tomorrow or the next day. They'll come here for him to recuperate. I tried to insist on going but . . . ' His voice wavered and he reached for her hands, holding them between his own.

'I'm so sorry. I know you want to be with them but your mother obviously thinks it's better you're here ready to help when they arrive.' She stared deep into his eyes. 'You want to disobey her, don't you?'

He gave a sheepish half-smile. 'Of course, wouldn't you?'

'Yes, but my mother's tough too and

would say the same sort of thing. It must be a pretty straightforward break if they're letting him go so soon.' She absently played with his fingers and sensed him relax a little.

'I know you're right, but it's still hard to sit back and do nothing.'

'Well, first you need to tell Caterina what's going on before she dies of curiosity, and then you must try to get some sleep. Your parents need you to be rested and able to take on whatever needs to be done in the morning.'

Gabe softly cradled her face in his large, strong hands. 'You're so special to me, Marianna, and one day I'll prove it to you.'

'Let's go in.' Right now she couldn't question too deeply what'd changed tonight between them. Maybe things would be clearer tomorrow.

★ ★ ★

After a disturbed night's sleep, Marianne showered, dressed and headed downstairs. Gabe's loud, forceful voice drifted up towards her and from the bottom step she watched him pace around the room, phone glued to his ear, rattling out instructions in rapid Italian. He finished and slammed the phone shut before noticing her and flashing a brief smile.

'Good news. Our private plane collected my parents a short while ago and they'll land within the hour. I wanted to pick them up from Catania but they insisted on having a company car come to the airport, so what could I do?' His expressive hands gestured defeat.

'Nothing much except what you were told. That's wonderful.' She hesitated. 'I've been thinking.' He interrupted before she could say any more.

'No. You are not leaving. You will not be in the way. There is plenty of room and my parents would be mortified if they thought they'd driven you away. In fact my mother can't wait to see you. They met Andy when they came to visit me in London years ago and loved him,' Gabe stated firmly.

'How did you know what I was going to say?' Marianne couldn't decide if she was thrilled or horrified at his intuition.

He grabbed hold of her shoulders and popped a light kiss on her forehead. 'You are a very polite, well-brought-up Englishwoman so I guessed the direction your mind had run in over the night, but you forgot one important thing.'

'What's that?'

'Two things actually. The first is the fact you're here as my guest and it would be extremely rude of me to ask you to leave, but most important is the fact I need you.' Gabe's voice dropped to a mere whisper against her warm cheek.

'I don't know what to say.'

His fingers pushed back through her freshly washed hair. 'Don't say anything. The first priority is breakfast. It'll be chaos when they arrive because my mama is like a tornado, so we need to be fortified. I told Caterina we will eat in the kitchen to make it easier for her if that's all right with you?'

'Of course.'

A few minutes later Marianne smiled at Gabe across the scrubbed pine table. His idea of a good breakfast was the typical Italian one consisting of a double shot of espresso and nothing else. The platters of cold meats, cheese, breads and pastries went untouched by him, but she was hungry yet again and loaded up her own plate.

'You're looking so much better than when you arrived last week,' he observed and she blushed again.

'After a month I'll be a blimp,' she tried to joke. 'I need to start running again.'

'The roads around here are quiet and safe. I've neglected my usual exercise routine too so I'll join you when things are more settled. Now if you'll excuse me I need to make some business calls before my parents arrive.' He stood and headed back out into the other room.

Marianne finished eating and took her dishes over by the sink. Caterina turned around and gave her a stern glare, so unlike her usual friendly smile it took her aback.

'Signor Dante is a good man and it is time he marry. I do not like Signorina Rossini much, but she is beautiful Italian lady who will give him lots of babies. You are not from here. You do not know our ways. A few weeks and you go home again.'

'Please don't worry. I have no intention of marrying Signor Dante or any other man,' Marianne tried to reassure her as tears pricked her eyes. She ran from the room and went upstairs, relieved to shut her bedroom door and find a moment's peace.

Foolish. That's what she was. She was sorry about Gabe's father but having his parents around could be her saving grace.

She changed into a simple, dark green linen dress, pairing it with new tan leather sandals she'd picked up in one of the local markets. Idly wasting time, she tidied up her bedroom and wrote a couple of postcards. After she heard a car arrive she lingered for a few more minutes before deciding she'd better head back down.

The house seemed full of noise, although when she walked into the living room she only saw Gabe and a glamorous older woman, who had to be his mother, chattering away loudly and gesticulating like crazy at the same time.

'Dante, you are a wicked boy.' The lady turned and walked towards Marianne. 'My dear. This son of mine did not tell me you are beautiful. No wonder he's disappointed we had to cut our holiday short.'

Gabe attempted to protest but gave up. 'Mamma, this is Marianna as if you hadn't already guessed.'

'Of course. As my son is too ignorant to introduce me, I am Sofia.' Her elegant hand reached out to tip up Marianne's chin, and dark inquisitive eyes that mirrored Gabe's studied her intently. 'I can see the resemblance to your dear brother. How is he?'

The question gave her breathing space and she rattled on about Andy's new bride and his job as a banker in Exeter. 'I was sorry to hear about Signor Alessandro. How is he doing?'

'I'm fine. Please come over here, as it's awkward for me to stand and greet you properly.'

She glanced towards the sofa at the man sat there and Marianne's heart did a funny sort of flip. This would be Gabe in another thirty years — tall, well dressed, his hair graying attractively at the temples, but still incredibly handsome and charismatic. Walking across she held out her hand and he took it lightly in his, planting a gentle kiss on her warm skin. The gesture made her smile.

'We do not stand on ceremony with our friends. You will call me Nico.'

'Thank you. Shouldn't you be resting?'

Sofia threw up her hands and launched into a tirade, clearly indicating she'd tried to make him but he wouldn't listen. Finally she slowed down. '*Scusa*, sorry, I should talk in English, but I am cross with him and when that happens I forget to be polite.'

Gabe sat by his father. 'Let's get you into bed. You are in the garden room at the back and I'll be next door.'

'But . . . '

'You can't manage the stairs with crutches so don't be stubborn. You know they only let you out because you were your usual argumentative self and insisted. We also have doctor's appointments set up for the next couple of months or so. You're doing what you are told for once.'

Sofia Alessandro broke into a broad smile. 'You see what a monster we created, Nico dear?' She looked directly at her husband and laughed. Gathering up a couple of overnight bags, she smiled at Marianne. 'I will see you later, my dear, after I've got this nuisance of a man settled.'

'Is there anything I can do to help?'

Gabe shook his head. 'Not right now but I'm sure there will be later.' He briefly took hold of her hand and Marianne couldn't pull away. 'Don't go anywhere.'

* * *

She fetched her book and wandered out onto the terrace. Under one of the shade trees framing the tiled outdoor area was a beautiful teak wood bench, perfectly situated to look out over the garden. For a while she forgot everything but the moment, relishing the fragrant scent of the exotic blossoms and allowing the book to fall to her side.

'There you are.' Gabe strolled towards her. 'Okay if I join you?'

'Of course. Whose house is it anyway?' she joked.

'I would not impose myself on you if

you wanted peace.'

Marianne patted the seat and encouraged him to sit down. 'I did think of something you need to do.'

'What's that?'

'Ring your aunt and uncle to cancel our weekend plans.'

His face dropped. 'Oh, I'd forgotten. I'm sorry.'

'Maybe we can go another time.'

A smile lightened his serious face. 'I hope so because you'd love it and we'd have fun together.'

She didn't answer for a moment, wondering if she'd had a lucky escape. 'Tell me about your father's leg. What did the doctors say?'

'He'll be in a cast for six to eight weeks and need X-rays every couple of weeks to make sure it's healing properly. Of course afterwards he'll need physical therapy to strengthen the leg again.' He picked up her hand idly, stroking it as he continued. 'Papa will be a terrible patient. He's never really been ill so I'm sure he'll make us all suffer. My parents argued about him trying windsurfing in the first place but he defied my mother and now she could strangle him.'

Marianne risked a smile, always lured to respond by his easy manner. 'He's a brave man to risk crossing her.'

'Or stupid depending on how you view things.'

'True.'

Gabe sighed. 'I can't stay any longer no matter how pleasant it is to be with you. I've got work to do.'

'I wish I could be more useful. I'm not used to being idle.'

'My dear girl.' Sofia Alessandro swept out onto the terrace. The smart white suit and heels she'd arrived in were now replaced by a vivid peacock-blue cotton dress and gold sandals. Her long black hair, dramatically streaked with white, was released from its previous elegant chignon and loosely caught back with large heavy gold clasps. 'I completely understand and do not worry. I will keep you occupied while my son sees to business. If Nico believes for a moment that he's being neglected he'll fret even more.'

'What do you have in mind, Mamma?' Gabe said warily.

'Run along and buy a hotel or something. This young lady and I will be fine, won't we?'

Marianne forced out a smile. 'Of course.'

Sofia shooed him away. 'Lunch will be at one. Your father should be awake by then. Thank goodness the pain medicine he took knocked him out before I did.'

Gabe nodded and walked away but behind his mother's back he caught Marianne's eye and flashed an overly dramatic grin. It took all her self-control to keep a straight face.

'Right. First I want you to come and help me carry some clothes down from our usual bedroom. While we do that you can tell me all about yourself.'

'Certainly.' The physical task wasn't a problem but she'd need to watch what she revealed to this shrewd woman.

For the next hour it wasn't hard to keep things simple because narrow spiral staircases didn't lend themselves to gossipy conversation.

'That will do for now.' Sofia finished organizing her assortment of expensive toiletries on the marble bathroom shelves and turned to Marianne with a satisfied smile. 'I've asked Caterina to bring us coffee on the terrace before we do anything else.'

It sounded like a command performance and Marianne dutifully followed as Signora Alessandro led the way.

'So, my dear. I understand from Dante you teach physical education to young people, is that correct?'

This was the easy part of her story and she purposely went into as much detail as possible, which wasn't hard because she genuinely loved her job.

'I admire you. I remember how difficult one teenage boy was to deal with and can't imagine a whole class full of them.' Sofia laughed.

'I'm sure it's different because they're not mine. Of course there're always one or two more challenging ones, but I usually manage to cope.'

The older woman threw her a piercing look. 'I have the impression you would not be easily cowed.'

'I hope not.' A lot hung unsaid between them and Marianne held her silence.

'What went wrong with your marriage?'

Marianne clutched her coffee cup and tried to hold her face in a polite half-smile, surprised at the sudden turn in the conversation. 'If you don't mind that's private and still very fresh. I'd rather not go into details. Robert wasn't the man I believed him to be and certain things occurred that made our marriage untenable.'

'I'm sorry, I didn't mean to upset you. Please forget I spoke.'

The only thing she was maybe genuinely sorry for was the fact she hadn't found out anything, but Marianne didn't blame her for being curious. 'That's all right.'

Caterina suddenly came out from the kitchen. 'Signor Nico is awake. I caught him limping out of the bedroom door. He was about to come out and look for you and I ordered him back to bed.'

Sofia's warm laughter pealed out. 'Well done. He's a naughty man and it will take all of us to get him well.' She stood up and faced Marianne. 'Don't hurry. Please take as long as you like and I will see you at lunch.'

Left alone everything flooded back, and the emotions she tried so hard to subdue overtook Marianne in painful sweeping waves. Would she never be free of Robert Blackwell?

'What on earth's wrong?' Gabe asked from the doorway, his face reflecting his obvious horror as he fixed on her distress.

8

Gabe strode across the room and pulled up a chair. He sat close to Marianne and gently wrapped his arms around her. 'Did my mother do something to upset you? If she did I'll . . . '

'No, it wasn't her. Well in a way it was, but it's hard to explain. She didn't mean any harm.' Marianne struggled to sound unconcerned but knew she failed by the worry etched into his face.

'I'm not so sure about that, but it's true she doesn't always think before she speaks.'

To calm herself down some more she started to tell him everything they'd done, including the pleasant conversation about her work, but when she came to the hard part the words tightened in her throat.

'If it upsets you to speak of it, please don't,' Gabe pleaded and as she met the concern in his warm eyes something opened in Marianne.

'I need to tell — if you don't mind?' Maybe he didn't want her confessions. For a second she nearly clammed up again.

'Say as much or as little as you want, *cara* Marianna. Is this about your marriage?'

She nodded and rested her head on the shoulder of his crisp white shirt, inhaling the fresh scent of air-dried cotton. 'What did Andy tell you?'

'Not much, honestly. He only said you'd been married but it didn't work and you divorced after six months. He didn't spell it out but I got the impression he hadn't liked your husband much.'

'That's true. Everyone else thought Robert was marvelous, but when we announced our engagement Andy wasn't pleased and asked if I was sure. Of course I didn't listen because I thought he was just doing his protective older brother thing.'

'I'd be the same if I had a sister,' Gabe declared vehemently, making Marianne laugh.

'No, you'd be worse.' she teased, but the moment of lightness faded. 'I've known Robert most of my life. We were at school together and then university. I'd always had a crush on him and was thrilled when he wanted to be more than friends. We got engaged and celebrated our wedding with all our family and friends. But things didn't go well afterwards.' The words dried in her throat and Marianne tried to look away but Gabe touched her chin bringing her back to his gaze. 'I knew he sometimes had a temper but he always said how much he loved me and I thought we'd be all right.'

'Did he harm you?' Anger etched in every line of Gabe's face, his mouth tight with suppressed emotion.

'Physically, no, but . . . ' She closed her eyes and the memories of Robert's attitude to her sent shivers down her spine. Gabe pulled her up against his warm chest and for a few moments she let herself be comforted by his steady heartbeat. 'It began with little comments about how much I ate and whether I'd soon be able to still fit into my clothes. We bought a house and every time I suggested a certain paint color or piece of furniture he'd question my taste. It shook my self-esteem so I ended up eating almost nothing, became convinced I couldn't do my job properly, and in the end I stopped doing everything he disapproved of because it was easier,' she whispered, barely holding back tears.

'How did you get the courage to leave?' Gabe murmured.

'We were visiting my parents and I fainted. I was put in the hospital because my weight was dangerously low. After a few weeks I was on the mend and allowed home. My parents kept Robert away until I was stronger.'

'What happened?'

'I insisted on seeing him, but only to say I wanted a divorce. He lost his temper and said some pretty terrible things which opened their eyes to what he was really like. The therapist told me it wasn't my fault, but I didn't believe her for a long while and still have days when I'm not sure.'

He eased away and gave her a fierce glare. 'Don't you ever say that again or think it. Do you hear me?'

'Yes, Gabe, I do.'

'I'm sorry, Marianna. You've had enough of a man telling you what to do and think.'

She reached over to rest her hand against his cheek. 'Oh, Gabe, it's completely different. I'm glad I've told you. Please don't tell your mother, all right?'

'Don't tell me what?' Sofia suddenly appeared, her sharp eyes darting from one to the other and checking them both out.

He quickly stood and kissed his mother on both cheeks. 'Nothing, Mamma, dear. Now tell me what's for lunch before I fade away completely.'

'You're a hopeless boy. Caterina's made your father's favorite fettuccini Alfredo followed by veal Milanese.'

'If he eats that way for the next six weeks he'll be enormous.' Gabe raised an eyebrow.

'Let him enjoy it. This isn't easy on him.'

'Or any of us,' he added almost under his breath.

'You take care of business, Dante, and I'll see to your father,' Sofia said firmly.

'Don't I always?' he replied, and Marianne wished she could fade into the background.

'That is quite enough. Please escort our guest in to lunch, and be careful what you say in front of your papa. I will not have him worried about anything, is that clear? His mood is bad enough already.' Sofia shook her head and swiveled away on her heels before walking briskly back inside.

'Sorry about this,' Gabe muttered quietly in her ear. 'In case you're wondering, it helps that you're here.'

She wasn't convinced but tried to give him a reassuring smile.

* * *

With lunch over and his parents retired to their room, Marianne sat across the table from Gabe and wondered what to say.

'Well, that was fun.' Gabe's sarcastic tone implied it definitely wasn't the case.

'Do you fancy a run later before dinner?' Marianne suggested. If she didn't do something active soon she'd explode.

'Why not? It'll have cooled off some by about six so we'll go then.'

They lapsed into silence.

'I expect you've got work to do.'

'Yes, but I don't feel like doing any,' Gabe said with a shrug. 'If I wasn't concerned about leaving the house for too long I'd suggest we get out of here, but there's nothing stopping you. Go shopping or whatever you like. You're supposed to be having a break.'

Marianne lightly smacked his arm. 'Don't patronize me.'

'Was I? I didn't mean to.' He looked surprised and she knew he'd only been trying to be kind.

'I'm considering taking a drive over to Trebellini. This should be a good time to catch Florenze.'

Gabe frowned. 'I thought we'd agreed to discuss it more over the weekend?'

'Did I?' she said with a touch of innocence. By his sardonic grin she guessed he wasn't fooled.

'You're a stubborn woman.'

'That's why you're entranced by me,' she teased, and Gabe's expression changed as he leaned closer and stroked his hand down her bare arm.

'Oh, Dante, I forgot to tell you . . . ' Sofia stood in the doorway, her face tight with disapproval. 'I've invited Alexandra for dinner tonight. She rang to ask how your papa was doing and told me she hadn't seen you for a week.'

'I've been busy. You know I was in Milan for three days,' Gabe said easily.

'Then I'm sure you'll be pleased to see her.' Sofia turned towards Marianne. 'Have you met Dante's fiancée?'

'Mamma, we're not engaged, I keep telling you that.' His exasperation burst through.

'We won't be saying that in front of your father tonight, will we?' The threat was clear.

Gabe sighed. 'No, Mamma.' He stood up and roughly pushed the chair away. 'Excuse me. I've got work to do.' Without waiting for an answer he strode from the room and closed the door behind him far louder than necessary.

Marianne prepared to make her escape too but Sofia placed her hand on the door knob. The force of her dark, narrow eyes pinned Marianne's feet to the ground. 'Do not abuse our hospitality. That is all I will say.'

There was so much she could say but

quickly decided silence was her best reply, so she held her tongue until Sofia gave up and took a step backwards. She headed for the spiral staircase, filled with a surge of energy. She'd get her keys and handbag and leave in the rental car. Maybe she wouldn't come back.

9

Several wrong turns, two narrow escapes from death-defying mopeds, and a close encounter with a herd of mangy sheep all combined to finish off Marianne. Driving into the next small town, she pulled into the first available parking space and turned off the engine, resting her head on the steering wheel, a hair's breadth from tears. Quickly she checked her mobile and almost cried with relief as a strong signal appeared.

'Oh, Gabe, thank goodness you're there.'

'You could've come upstairs and found me.' He sounded puzzled. 'What can I do for you?' Humor hummed through his voice.

'I'm an idiot.'

'What's happened?' Before she could answer he spoke again. 'Where are you anyway? I'm guessing not in the house?'

'I'm not sure, but I think the sign said Randazzo.'

Gabe's raucous laughter echoed down the line. 'How the devil did you get there?'

'I thought I remembered the way to Trebellini, but I guess I didn't.' Her voice faded away.

'Don't worry, *cara*, it's all right. Are you parked on the piazza?'

'I think so. There's a strange dark-colored church in front of me.'

'Good. That's the Chiesa di Santa Maria. Do you see a café called Delizioso to your right?'

'Yes.'

'Lock up the car and go and wait there. I'll be about an hour. If Antonio's around I'll bring him with me and he'll return your car back to the garage, if that's okay with you?'

She managed a small laugh. 'I think that might be wise.'

'I'll let Mamma know where I'm going then we'll be on our way.'

'Do you have to tell her? She doesn't have a high opinion of me now and this'll make it worse. She'll say I've done it on purpose to lure you away,' Marianne said ruefully.

'I'll tell her your car broke down.'

'You are far too accomplished a liar, Dante Gabriel Alessandro.'

'Not when it's important,' he stated quietly.

'Well, thank you anyway.'

'It's not a problem.' Gabe chuckled. 'It doesn't look good for the family's reputation if we lose a guest.'

'You couldn't resist that, could you?'

'Not really. *Ciao*, darling girl.'

He hung up before she could tell him off any more.

★ ★ ★

Marianne sipped an ice-cold Orangina and gazed around at the pretty little town. She wasn't sure why the sight of clean washing strung from balconies around the streets looked charming when at home it'd strike her as messy. Small groups of old men stood around talking and smoking while putting the world to rights, and short, stocky women dressed all in black bustled along doing their daily shopping. At a sudden loud noise people around her turned to look at something. She leaned forward and craned her neck to see what was so interesting. She should've guessed.

'I didn't have a white horse available to rescue you so I hope this will do?' Gabe stopped his flashy black Alfa Romeo right in front of her and leapt out. Antonio Palmetto emerged from the passenger door, his face a mixture of embarrassed and pleased. 'Give me your keys and I'll get Antonio on his way.'

She tried to thank the older man but he merely gave a brief nod and clutched at the cap he'd hastily pulled off his head to greet her. Gabe took him to her car and five minutes later was back. Of course the waitress immediately rushed over, but didn't all women where he was concerned?

'Ah, that's better.' He drained his Coke in a couple of large swallows. 'So are you all right?' Gabe picked up her hands.

Marianne froze. 'I was, but we won't be in a minute.'

'What on earth do you mean?'

'Signorina Westlake. Signor Alessandro. What a surprise to see you both here. Together.' Florenze Giovanni stood, arms on hips, glaring straight at them.

'It's a surprise to see you too. I can explain.' Marianne stumbled over her words but Gabe took her hand and shook his head.

'It's my place to do that.' He gestured to one of the empty chairs at the small table. 'Join us, Florenze, please.' Quickly he got them more drinks. 'Signorina Westlake is an old friend of the family. She came for a visit and I asked her to help me with a problem regarding the Bella Rosa.' He hesitated, glancing first at a glowering Florenze and then back at Marianne. 'We've suspected for a while all isn't well in the way the hotel's being run.'

'In what way?'

Marianne's stomach turned. If the girl didn't plead her case she'd be in as much trouble as the rest of the staff. Gabe might prefer to do this alone, but she owed Florenze the chance to redeem herself. 'I think you know what we're talking about. My first night with you an extra salad and glass of wine were added to the bill.' The girl's face flushed bright crimson and she clutched her hands on her lap, still not saying anything. 'The next evening an inflated tip was added to my credit card bill after I'd signed.'

'Florenze, Signorina Westlake is convinced you didn't want to be involved but says the Galasso family has a hold over you. Is this true?'

Now the furious glare focused on Marianne. 'You promised,' Florenze snapped.

'I'm sorry.'

'We both want to help but we need your cooperation.' Gabe tried to smooth the waters.

'What if I don't?' Florenze paled under her olive skin.

Gabe squeezed Marianne's hand to stop her from answering. 'Then I'm afraid I'll have to conclude you were a willing partner and deal with you accordingly.' His face softened. 'I don't want that. Apart from anything else your aunt and uncle are very dear to me and it would upset them greatly.'

Florenze's glance dropped down to her lap and slow tears trickled down her face. 'All right. I'll tell you everything. I have no choice.'

They listened quietly to the sad tale of fleecing customers, double sets of books for the accountant, supplies sold from the back door to neighboring businesses, all started because Enrico Galasso was a greedy unscrupulous man. 'He did it because he could. Your father trusted him and let him run the hotel without much supervision.'

Florenze snorted. 'He wasn't the only one fooled. Many people believe Galasso is a good man.' She looked directly at Gabe. 'I'm very sorry. I shouldn't have helped them. It was wrong of me.'

'You had your reasons.' Marianne tried to make it more acceptable, but the girl shook her head.

'That does not make it right and you know it.' She sounded disappointed with herself.

Gabe spoke up. 'Are you working tonight?'

'No, I'm over here to visit my cousin. I will be back for breakfast service.'

'I want you to ring the hotel in the morning and say you are sick and will not be in all day tomorrow. I'm coming to tackle Signor Galasso and don't want you to be there.'

Marianne touched his hand. 'What about your father?'

'His first hospital appointment isn't until Friday. I told him yesterday what we'd found out. He wants it resolved and worries because he feels responsible, so the faster I can sort it the better.' He turned to Florenze. 'Is that all right with you?'

She shrugged. 'It has to be.'

'What will you do?' Marianne asked.

'Leave. I cannot stay.'

'What about your English classes and the training you need to go to Rome?'

'That will have to wait.'

Gabe interrupted. 'I could help you out with that.'

Her stony face was rigid with disgust. 'I will not be bribed. I have taken enough of your money already.'

Marianne squeezed Gabe's hand before he could say any more. 'We understand. We're very sorry it's ended this way.'

'Yes, well, that is life. I will survive.' She got up and walked away.

Before Gabe could say anything more Marianne glanced around at the other customers and back to him with a smile. He got the hint and kept his mouth shut. 'How about a walk around before we go back?' She craved a little time with him before his family and Alexandra took him from her again, even though it was probably unwise.

'It will be all right, Marianna.'

She pushed back tears and gave a brilliant smile. 'Of course it will.' He'd misunderstood, but maybe that was just as well.

'Come on.' He stood and held out his hand which she took without hesitation.

For the next hour Marianne pushed everything else from her mind but the here and now and sensed him do the same. They explored the fascinating black church they'd used earlier as a landmark, made of local lava stone, like much of the town. They skipped the other churches, choosing to walk around the remains of the old medieval walls and have a quick look at the castle.

'It's too grim for today, *tesoro*, my sweetheart. I think we can do without torture chambers and a well used for burying people alive, don't you?'

Marianne screwed up her face in disgust. 'Thanks for telling me. Now I'll have bad dreams tonight.' He pulled her into his arms and his hands rested at the base of her spine. She didn't want to investigate too hard why being with Gabe always felt so right. 'We'd better go.' Saying nothing in reply, he only nodded and took her hand. Very quietly they got in the car and drove in silence back to the house.

Before she could step out of the car he put his hand on her arm. 'Don't believe everything you hear tonight, please.'

Caterina appeared at the door as she always did so Marianne didn't make any comment, merely gave a small smile and went inside. She headed straight upstairs and prepared to stay there until it was time for dinner. She'd need all her resolve to face the evening ahead.

* * *

There was no point trying to compete with two glamorous Italian women, one of whom was a top runway model. Marianne chose white linen wide-legged trousers topped with a raspberry-pink silk camisole, no jewelry, and a pair of simple white sandals. With her newly tanned skin and a touch of pink lip gloss she felt better than she'd done in a very long time. One quick spritz of light floral perfume and she was as ready as she'd ever be.

'Marianne, my dear, come over here with the ladies while our dreadful men talk business as usual,' Sofia called out the moment she walked into the room. 'Alexandra's been telling me all about the modeling shoot she did today over in Taormina. Have you been there yet?'

She nearly put her foot in her mouth but managed to stop herself just in time. Admitting that she and Gabe had planned a weekend there wasn't a wise idea. 'No, but I've heard it's very beautiful.'

'Oh, it is.' Sofia happily chattered away until Caterina announced dinner was served on the terrace. 'Now we're splitting you men up so you can't bore us with talk of stocks and shares all evening. Dante, you're over here by Alexandra. Marianne, I know Nico wants to get to know you better so you can sit between us.'

She smiled, determined not to show any concern over Sofia's blunt effort to separate her from Gabe. It wasn't any hardship to talk to his father anyway and he made her laugh with stories of Gabe's childhood and all the scrapes he'd got into.

When the coffee arrived Sofia instantly stood up and apologized. 'We'll take ours in our room if you don't mind. Nico is tired and needs to rest.' She glanced around the table. 'We'll leave you young people alone.'

Nico balanced on his crutches again and walked around the table, stopping between Gabe and Alexandra. 'It does me good to see you two together. Son, I hope you'll be giving us some good news soon?'

Marianne dropped her gaze to the table unable to watch him lie, but at the last second looked over, shaken by his calm open smile.

'I hope so too, Papa.' He rested his hand tenderly on Alexandra's arm.

It was far too convincing and made her realize she knew very little about this man. Who was to say this was the lie and the closeness they'd shared the truth? Briefly their eyes met and she registered his disappointment with her reaction. He could just be disappointed. She wasn't opening herself up to be hurt by any man again. Marianne gave a deliberate yawn. 'It's been a long day. I believe I'll give coffee a miss and have an early night.'

'Please don't leave on our account.' Alexandra held Gabe's hand in a deliberate gesture of possession.

Marianne gritted her teeth. 'I'm not, I can assure you. It's been a pleasure to meet you again and do enjoy the rest of the evening.'

'I'm sure we will, won't we, Dante?'

The woman practically purred and Marianne struggled to drag up a friendly smile. Gabe merely muttered what might've been agreement and turned his head away slightly to look out over the sea.

'Good night.' Sleep would surely be a long time coming tonight, but she'd endured enough restless nights recently to know it wouldn't kill her. Tomorrow she'd be stronger where Dante Gabriele Alessandro was concerned. Soon she'd be back to her normal life and everything would be fine.

Who she thought she was fooling Marianne wasn't sure.

10

With a sense of relief Marianne watched from an upstairs window as Gabe's car pulled out through the wrought-iron gates. She'd purposely avoided going down for breakfast, not wanting to face anybody after last night's little show. Pulling on her running shoes, she checked the laces were tight before heading to the kitchen to fill up her water bottle.

'Ah, Marianne, we wondered where you were.' Sofia stopped talking to Caterina and turned around.

'I'm afraid I overslept.' She wished it were true but uninterrupted nights were a thing of the past where she was concerned. 'I'm off out for a run.'

Sofia frowned. 'Without any breakfast?'

'I prefer to eat when I return.'

'Is it safe on your own?'

'Gabe assured me the roads are quiet around here so I'm sure I'll be fine.' Marianne went over to the sink and turned on the cold tap, relieved the water up here on the mountain was good so it wasn't necessary to drink bottled water all the time. 'I'll be back within an hour.' She left before she could be interrogated any more.

Warm air, a slight breeze off the mountain, and not a soul in sight. This was perfect. Marianne completely got into the zone and concentrated on her technique, first building up speed and then maintaining a steady pace as she made her way around the circular route Gabe suggested. As the villa came into sight she began to slow and finally stopped outside to do her usual cool-down stretches before pressing the gate buzzer to be let back in. Not wanting to go into the house straightaway she wandered around to the terrace at the back.

'Hello, my dear. What a pleasant surprise.' Nico leaned forward from where he sat on the bench, his crutches propped up against a nearby lemon tree.

'I'm sorry, I didn't mean to interrupt your rest.'

'Please do. Sofia is taking the doctor's instructions so literally. I'm surprised I'm allowed to breathe. It's a broken leg not a heart attack, although to hear her you'd think I was going to die tomorrow.'

His gentle smile reminded her so much of Gabe it was hard to form a reply. 'At a guess I'd say she knows you're a man who'll try to rush getting back to normal, which won't work with this injury.'

Nico gave an easy shrug and grinned. 'You're right. It's hard when you're used to being active.' He patted the space next to him. 'Come and join me.'

Marianne sat and opened up her water bottle to take a deep swallow. They settled into an easy conversation about her run and went on to discuss the garden. Nico's deep love and wide knowledge of plants were a surprise to her coming from this suave, urbane man.

'I think I'd like to have a garden one day although I always avoided ours at home when my dad tried to get me interested.'

'I thought all Englishwomen were expert gardeners?' he asked with a teasing smile.

'I obviously missed that gene.'

'You can help Antonio out anytime. His English isn't wonderful but I'm pretty sure a weed is a weed in any language.' He studied her hard from under his slightly hooded dark eyes. 'It'd give you something to do.'

This man knew she wasn't a girl to be idle, exactly as his son had. 'I'd love to if I wouldn't be a nuisance.'

Nico rested his warm hand on hers for a moment. 'A beautiful woman can never be that.'

Marianne grinned. 'I see now where Gabe gets his charming manners from. You Italian men are all the same. Totally unbelievable, but irresistible anyway.'

He gave her a very shrewd look. 'Don't be fooled. Under the surface we are very deep and truthful but not everyone digs down that far.'

There was no suitable answer without saying things she wasn't about to let out of her mouth. 'I need to go and shower. If you'll excuse me.' She stood before he could delay her with more probing words and felt his gaze follow her as she walked away. She had to wonder what he'd really meant. Life in the Alessandro house wasn't the restful experience she'd expected and she couldn't decide whether that made her happy or worried.

'Ah, there you are, Marianne.' Sofia looked up from the letter she was writing, as always the picture of elegance. Today she was dressed in deep purple and seated at a charming antique desk in the corner of the room. 'You missed a telephone call while you were out. Andy phoned.'

'Oh, what a pity. I'll call him later.'

Sofia frowned. 'He said for you to phone him immediately you got back. I am to tell you everybody is fine but he has some news you need to hear.' She looked questioningly at Marianne, obviously expecting an explanation, but there wasn't one to give because she hadn't a clue what he'd meant. 'Please feel free to use the phone in Nico's office.'

'Thanks, but I've got my mobile upstairs so it's not a problem.' She left and headed up, wondering whether to shower first before deciding if Andy had said immediately that's what he meant. Her brother wasn't one to fuss.

Turning on the phone, she took a deep breath before entering his number. He answered on the first ring, making her pretty certain he'd been waiting.

'I'm glad you weren't too long. Only I've got to meet a client in a few minutes.'

'What's wrong? I love talking to you but I'm sure you didn't call in the middle of a work day to see how I am.'

'Not exactly.' Andy hesitated. 'It's awkward. Mum and Dad think I'm worrying too much, but Janet agreed with me and thought I should call.'

'Get on with it, big brother. Surely it can't be that bad?'

'It's about Robert.'

Marianne's stomach churned and she sunk down onto the bed.

'He's resigned from his job, sold the house and disappeared.'

'But what's that to me? I don't care where he is.'

'What if he's in Sicily?'

A laugh choked in Marianne's throat. 'Why on earth would you think that?'

'Maybe the fact I bumped into his brother and Philip told me his suspicions. Robert stayed with their parents a few nights, then left with a suitcase and his passport without saying where he was going. Philip found travel brochures for Sicily in the rubbish bin in Robert's bedroom.' Andy's voice deepened in anger. 'If he . . . '

'Yes, I know what you'd do and so would Gabe.'

'Gabe? How does he know about any of this?'

'I told him.' She heard her brother's quick intake of breath. 'I didn't plan to but it came out one evening when we were alone.' Even over the phone she sensed Andy's eyebrows rise in a question. 'If you're right, how did he know I'm here?' She'd told no one outside of the family and sworn them to secrecy.

'I can't be sure but my best guess, and she denies this,is: I know Mum met Robert's mother out shopping the other day and I'm guessing it slipped out when they were talking. Look, Marianne, I've got to go but promise me you'll be very careful. Don't go out alone and if you've trusted Gabe this much already please share this with him so he can watch out too.'

She caught the worry in his voice. 'I'll be careful.'

'What about Gabe?'

'Let me think about it.' There was too much Andy didn't know about where her awkward relationship with Gabe was concerned. 'How about I email you each day to let you know I'm still alive?' She forced out a laugh.

'You do that. Bye for now.'

Marianne held on to the empty phone for a long time.

* * *

Back downstairs she gave in to Caterina's insistence and ate some breakfast. Fresh sweet melon, a delicious almond pastry, frothy cappuccino and the wonderful view from her chair on the patio — it all restored her equilibrium. Terraces of vines clung to the steep hillside while picturesque villages and clusters of goats all led down to the distant, sparkling azure-blue sea. Right now the thought of returning to Plymouth wasn't at all enticing.

'There you are.' Gabe strode across

the terrace, a broad smile lighting up his handsome face. 'I thought you'd like to know what happened this morning.'

For a moment she stared at him blankly, then it came back to her. 'Oh, the hotel. Sorry it slipped my mind. I've been for a run and spent some time talking to your father.' She avoided mentioning Andy's call and crossed her fingers no one else would've told him. 'How did it go? Worse than expected?'

He gave a wry smile and shrugged. 'I didn't have high expectations so wasn't disappointed. Enrico Galasso gave me the usual hot denials before it turned into profuse apologies and rather humiliating pleading to be allowed to stay.'

Marianne couldn't drag her eyes away from him, happy to watch his strong, tanned hands tell stories for ever in that uniquely Italian way.

'That all came before I fired him, at which point it turned to abuse and curses on my family.' Gabe grinned.

'Pretty much a run-of-the mill morning.'

'I'm sorry it came to this. What about his son and the rest of the staff?'

'I fired Philippe. He was in on the whole thing with his father, plus it's obvious he can't cook. I'm keeping the other staff for now although I've warned them all. I'm bringing in my friend Andrea to be the manager. He's looking for somewhere smaller to run after many years of working large hotels so I think it'll suit him perfectly.' He lowered his voice. 'I've spoken to Florenze. I've offered her the chance to come back as Andrea's assistant and continue her college classes.'

'What did she say?'

He frowned. 'She wants to think about it. She's still hung up on the fact she didn't speak up before and sees this as an undeserved reward.'

'If I'm interfering, say so, but would it be of any help it I talked to her?'

'It can't hurt. Would you mind?'

'Not at all. Have you told your father all this?'

Gabe smiled. 'Yes, and funnily enough it made him feel better — to be involved again I suppose. He's cross he didn't see the problems before but seems pleased with my solution.'

'What about a chef?'

'I'm advertising already, but until then I'm giving Mario, who's been working under Philippe, a chance. I've put him on a month's trial.' Suddenly he reached across the table and picked up Marianne's hands. 'I've got you to thank for all this. It would've been a lot harder to prove without your help.'

She flushed hotly. 'I didn't do much.'

'Yes, you did, and I know it wasn't easy on several levels.'

Marianne was relieved he didn't say any more because her feelings about the whole episode with Florenze were still very mixed.

'About last night,' Gabe murmured softly.

She wished he'd stop massaging her skin with his long fingers. For this conversation she needed to think straight. Pointedly she pulled away and planted her hands firmly on her lap.

'I behaved the way I did to pacify my father, which may be wrong but I couldn't upset him when he's in pain.'

'So are you going to walk down the aisle with Alexandra to keep him happy too? It's none of my business, Gabe, but surely at some point he needs to know the truth — if it is the truth?' Marianne challenged him.

'Don't you believe me?'

'Why does it matter whether I do or not?' He stared into her, his dark eyes almost black with emotion and it took all her strength not to waver.

'I believe you know the answer even if I'm not supposed to say it out loud. You're an intelligent woman, Marianne. You tell me why it's important.'

She jumped up. 'I can't deal with all this right now, as you well know. You need to sort out your personal life for your own sake. It's nothing to do with me.'

He stood too and grabbed her hands again, holding on firmly. 'But it is . . . '

Marianne knew she needed to put a stop to this right now. 'No, Gabe, it mustn't be. Do it for yourself and for Alexandra — you're not being fair on her. It's time your parents understood you're a grown man and will make your own decisions. Trust me, your father will survive if you don't marry the woman he'd prefer for you.'

Gabe's expression hardened. 'I agree, but now isn't the right time.'

'You could make excuses for ever.'

'Is your opinion of me so low?' He looked bewildered and hurt.

'Certainly not. You're a decent man who loves his family and has sacrificed a lot for them. Your loyalty does you credit, but maybe you carry it too far.' Impulsively she reached up and pressed a soft kiss on his cheek. 'You've been more than kind to me too, and I do appreciate it.'

'That's easy.' He trailed one finger down the side of Marianne's face, sending a shiver of delight all the way to her toes. She shouldn't want him to kiss her but . . .

'Dante, there's a phone call for you inside and Marianne, did you manage to speak to Andy all right?' Sofia stared at them both, her expression loaded with disapproval.

'Thank you, Mamma, I'll be right in.' He glanced back at Marianne. 'You didn't say Andy rang.'

'I hadn't got around to it.' In a split second decision she chose to trust her instinct. 'I've got a message for you from him but it can wait until later.' Hopefully he'd get the hint she wasn't about to discuss it in front of his mother. The touch of a smile tugging at his mouth told her he did and she felt absurdly pleased.

'I'll look forward to hearing it. I've been thinking recently how I miss his friendship.' He squeezed her hands tightly, ignoring his mother's glare.

'Excuse me for now.'

Marianne turned calmly towards Sofia. 'Andy was fine, thank you, and sends his regards to you all. He was just being the protective older brother and checking I was all right.' She really didn't care if she was believed. 'I think I'll go and read my book until lunchtime.' She walked away feeling the other woman's gaze directed right at her back, but she didn't look around. Let her wonder.

11

'Do you fancy a walk into Pozzala, Marianna?' Gabe asked as they finished up dinner.

'That'd be lovely.' Plus it'd give them a chance to talk without his mother watching them like the proverbial hawk.

'Isn't Alexandra coming over?'

Gabe winced at his mother's pointed question, the muscles in his jaw tightening to a stern line. 'Not tonight. She's busy.'

'When are you seeing her again?'

'I'm not sure. Please leave it up to us. We're not children.'

Nico scowled. 'Dante, there is no need to be rude to your mother.'

'I'm sorry, but at thirty-one years old I don't expect to be questioned like a teenage boy either,' he stated firmly and Marianne held her breath.

The two men's eyes met and both

held their ground for what seemed like an eternity before Nico conceded and looked away. 'Sorry, my boy, I didn't mean to push. I've watched Alexandra grow up into a beautiful, accomplished woman and I truly thought she would be an excellent partner for you in life. Maybe I was wrong.'

'No, you were not, Nicolo Giovanni,' Sofia snapped. 'They are a perfect couple and Dante was all set to formalize things until Marianne arrived.'

'That's quite enough, Mamma. How dare you embarrass our guest this way?' Gabe's features darkened in anger. 'My relationship with Alexandra is between the two of us and I'll be talking with her very soon. Afterwards I'll let you know exactly what's happening, but until then it is not up for discussion.'

Marianne's heart raced and she thought she might faint. Suddenly Gabe seized hold of her hand and practically pulled her up to standing.

'Let's go.' He gave his parents a tight smile. 'We'll see you later.'

Before she could consider protesting he raced them from the room. 'I need to change my shoes. These aren't suitable for walking down the hill.' She pointed to her thin strappy sandals.

'Fine, I'll wait outside.' His tone didn't invite any argument.

Only when they were nearly down to the town did Gabe's brisk pace ease. She considered herself fit but it'd taken all her stamina to keep up with him. 'Finished the marathon, have we?' she teased, relieved when he turned back and flashed one of his winning smiles.

'Sorry. I needed to work off some frustration. I'll make it up to you by buying you the best ice cream you'll ever taste.'

She laughed. 'Do you really think I'm that easy, Dante Gabriele Alessandro?'

Turning around he placed his hands on her shoulders, pressing slightly and making her aware of his controlled strength. 'No, Marianna. If you were I wouldn't be so fascinated by you.'

Too stunned to reply, she tried to

ease away but he wouldn't let her move. After several long moments of staring deeply into her eyes he rested his warm lips lightly on her forehead.

'Cassata Siciliana with mascarpone, candied fruit and nuts. I'll order for us.' His husky voice betrayed him and she thought she was grateful when he let go and walked towards the café, but couldn't be sure.

For a while they simply enjoyed eating the delicious creamy treat and watching the life going on around them.

'Tell me about Andy's call,' Gabe asked, gently picking up one of her hands and cradling it in his own, his warmth and nearness allowing her to relax slightly. She recited all the details and noticed the increasing tension, both in his face and in the way his fingers tightened around hers.

'I'm sure he's being overly concerned. The divorce is final. There's no reason for Robert to follow me here. What's the point?'

'Did he willingly agree to the divorce?'

She frowned, unsure quite how much to say, but in the end couldn't hold back. 'Yes and no. He was vehemently against it until my father had a word with him about the way he'd treated me.' She watched the wheels turn in Gabe's head before he spoke again, smiling inside at his obvious care for her feelings.

'I'm not trying to tell you what to do, but I'd suggest not being out on your own while you're here.'

'He's not going to make me a prisoner. The main reason I agreed to come here in the first place was to get away from the whole unpleasant aftermath of my marriage,' Marianne protested.

'Nobody wants to make you one. Would you be agreeable to putting me on the speed dial of your phone so it'll be easy to keep in contact? Also, how about you promise to let one of us know where you're going and roughly how long you think you'll be?'

The tentative suggestions made sense but part of her still wanted to rile against them. She made herself stop and really think hard before replying. 'All right. I suppose it's the best compromise. I'll let Andy know so he might stop being such a worry-head.'

'Do you mind if I get in touch with him too? Partly to reassure him you're being taken care of, but more because I'd simply like to,' Gabe asked.

She nodded. 'It'd be good for you both and anyway he might think I'm making it all up. I've done that before.' Her smile faded. 'Especially during my marriage when I didn't want anyone to know how bad things were and what a fool I'd been to be taken in by a handsome face.'

Gabe moved his hands up to her shoulders and the slight pressure forced her to look directly at him. 'Don't be so harsh on yourself. We all make errors of judgment.' He flashed a quick smile. 'Even I'm not perfect you know.'

'Really? I'd never have guessed.' Being with him was so easy and the constant battle against giving in to his appeal got harder by the hour.

He lowered his hands and picked up the glass of sparkling water he'd abandoned, taking a long swallow before glancing back at her. 'I'm meeting Alexandra tomorrow for lunch.'

What was she supposed to say? 'That's nice.'

'Nice? I doubt it. She won't be happy when I've finished, let's put it that way, but it's got to be done.'

The inference was obvious but she was wary of asking him to spell it out because of where the conversation might go next.

'Well, aren't you going to say anything?' He fixed her with those darkest of dark eyes.

'Like what? Congratulations for doing what you should've done a long time ago? You don't need my approval or otherwise. I'll be gone in a few weeks so does it really matter what I think?'

'If you insist on being obtuse, go ahead. We both know what's happening between us, but you're not ready to admit it.' He waved his hands in a gesture of dismissal. 'I understand, I really do, Marianna. You've recently got out of a bad marriage, you don't trust your own judgment and it'll take time to overcome. I know you need friends at the moment more than anything, but it's hard for me to pretend indifference.' Gabe leaned closer and his warm breath caressed her skin. 'Marianna.' He pulled away, his voice gruff. 'I will try to be a gentleman for both our sakes.'

'I'm sorry.'

'Don't be, my love. You can't help being beautiful and adorable.' He laughed and ruffled her hair in a faux-friendly way. 'I think we'd better go before I drag you into a dark alley and have my wicked way with you.' He grimaced. 'Of course I'd have my father, yours, and Andy after me if I tried something so crass.'

Marianne didn't usually have this kind of effect on men. The reality of marriage with Robert hadn't been what she'd imagined but she sensed things would be totally different with Gabe. *What on earth was she thinking?*

'Come on,' he encouraged.

The pleasant stroll back up the hill went by too quickly and they entered the house to a scene of noisy chaos. In the entrance hall Nico yelled at a red-faced Sofia, trying to gesticulate with his hands while balancing on his crutches. Marianna took a step backwards, shaken by the sense of anger filling the air. Hearing Robert's name mentioned, she started to tremble and Gabe's arm slipped around her waist.

'It's all right. They don't mean anything by it. They'll make up later, trust me,' he whispered in an attempt to reassure her.

'I want to go to my room,' Marianne pleaded.

'Of course, come on. We'll leave them alone.' He steered her around the warring couple and up the spiral staircase. Opening her bedroom door he followed her in and closed the door behind them. 'Shall we sit on your balcony for a while?' Without waiting for an answer he opened the interior glass door first and then the metal one leading out to the small balcony overlooking the garden. Gabe dropped down to sit on one of the white wood chairs and pulled her onto his lap.

'I'm sorry to be such a . . . '

He silenced her with a finger pressed to her lips. 'Don't apologize. We Mediterranean people thrive on noisy fights, but then it's all forgotten and we're friends again. You English aren't exactly the same, are you?'

'It's not that and you know it,' she retorted.

'You don't need to apologize either. It's not your fault your ex-husband wasn't a good person. That's his problem not yours, which I hope one day you'll really believe.'

'Will I? I wonder sometimes. Some

days I think I'll never be free of the past.' She'd never spoken her fears out loud before.

'The past is part of us. It's how we deal with it which determines the future. Do you know what I think?'

His tender smile broke through one of the walls she'd built around her heart for her own protection. 'What?'

'You're a strong woman. You must be to have come through all this as well as you have. Be kind to yourself and patient. One day this will only be a small part of who you are.'

'I hope you're right.'

Gabe flashed a wide white-toothed smile. 'Of course I am. No question. Now I think you've had enough for one day. How about you get ready for bed and if you're very good I'll tuck you in. If you're extra lucky you'll get one very chaste, respectable kiss.'

She teasingly screwed up her face. 'Only one?'

'Yes, Marianna, only one,' he stated very forcefully. 'Up you get and run in and do whatever you women do before bed.'

Marianne hopped up from his lap.

'I'll stay here until you give me the all-clear.' He stared straight out into the darkness while she left.

Soon she lay in bed and pulled the sheet up before calling to Gabe. He came in from the balcony, carefully locking the doors behind him. Leaning over he gave her a very quick kiss on her forehead.

'Don't ask for any more.'

'I wouldn't dare.' Which was the truth. 'One thing before you leave, Gabe.'

'Oh, Marianna, take pity on me please.' He turned around as he headed towards the door and his wry grin made her smile.

'When you discover what your parents were arguing about will you tell me?'

'If it's something you need to know, of course I will.'

'Do you mean it?' She wasn't stupid.

She'd caught Robert's name in the middle of the screeching tirade downstairs and was sure he did too. Very deliberately she stared into Gabe's eyes and he met her gaze straight on, never flinching.

'Yes, I promise. I won't ever lie to you.'

'That's a big promise to make and you know it's hard for me to believe, don't you?'

'I'll convince you one day.' With one quick smile he left.

Marianne sighed. So much for Andy's bright idea of her escaping to Sicily for a peaceful retreat from life.

12

'Is Signor Dante around, Caterina?'
Marianne asked as she buttered a slice
of toast and poured a mug of fresh
coffee, trying to sound only vaguely
interested.

'No, Signorina. He's gone to the
hotel in Trebellini this morning and
then he meet Signorina Alexandra for
lunch. He say to tell you he will be back
for dinner.'

'What about his parents?'

Caterina's face set into a stony mask
and her lips formed a tight line.
'Signora Sofia is out shopping and
Signor Nico is in his room.'

Plainly there'd been no making up
yet. 'Signor Dante said your husband
might let me help in the garden.' She
needed something to occupy the
morning.

The older woman frowned. 'He not

say anything to us, but I suppose you can.' Her gaze swept over Marianne's short white dress. 'You wear that?'

'No, don't worry, I'll go and change into some old clothes.' Marianne laughed and put her dishes by the sink and ran off upstairs. Digging in the dirt had to be better than sitting around worrying.

★ ★ ★

Completely engrossed in trying to remember which she'd been told were weeds to pull and which were plants, Marianne was startled when Nico suddenly spoke near her shoulder.

'Well, we'll make a gardener of you yet.' Gabe's father smiled broadly down at her kneeling in the flower bed.

'I'm not sure it's very likely.' She pushed a strand of hair out of her sweaty face and wiped her neck off with a handkerchief from her pocket. 'I think I scare poor Antonio. Caterina gave him instructions so he brought me out here, pointed at a few things, pushed this shovel and bucket at me and walked off as fast as he could. Every now and then he comes and checks on me, mutters a little more, and disappears again.

'You look hot. How about a cold drink?'

'I'd love one but I can't go into the kitchen like this, Caterina would have a fit.' She pointed to the film of dirt stuck to her damp, hot skin.

'I'll ask her to bring some lemonade out,' Nico asserted.

'Oh, please don't. I don't want her to think I'm some sort of diva.'

He gave one of the ultra-charming smiles so like Gabe's it made her melt inside. 'I'll tell her it's for the invalid and you're keeping me company so need some too. Don't run off.' Hobbling away he headed for the kitchen door.

Marianne stood and wiped off her hands as best she could on her denim shorts then walked over to sit down, grateful for the shade and to get a break for her sore knees.

Five minutes later Nico made his way back across the grass, followed by Caterina carrying a large tray which she set on the low teak table in front of the bench.

Immediately her steely gazed fixed on Marianne. 'Here, Signorina, wash.'

A soapy flannel from one bowl was pushed into her hands. She dutifully got most of the grime off then was pointed towards another bowl of clean water before being handed a towel.

'Much better.' Caterina nodded her approval and muttered something to Nico.

'She says you look more like a lady again now,' he translated.

'Instead of what, or shouldn't I ask?' Marianne joked.

'Don't ask.' He grinned and turned to thank the older woman. Caterina promptly gave him more instructions before returning to the house. 'She says I am not to stay too long, it is too hot and I should have my leg up resting more or I will never walk properly again and it will serve me right.'

'She's brutal.'

'She's a woman,' he said dryly. 'I'm used to them ordering me around.'

Marianne had to smile. 'I'll bet you don't always obey though without protest.'

'Last night for instance?'

She glanced away from his perceptive look and concentrated on choosing an almond croissant from the selection which had arrived with the drinks. It hadn't been her intention to bring up the subject but she'd keep going with it and see what she could find out. 'Remember I don't speak Italian so I don't know what you were discussing and it's none of my business, is it?' A slight flush tinged his cheeks and she knew she'd been right.

'I was not happy with my wife.'

'Really? I'd never have guessed.' She was tired of talking delicately around the subject. 'Did I hear my ex-husband's name mentioned?'

Nico turned directly towards her. 'Yes, you did, and that's what we were arguing about. There was a phone call while you and my son were out. Sofia answered and a man asked to speak to you. She told him you'd be back later and offered to take a message but he declined. After she put down the phone and told me who it was I lost my temper. Dante told us your ex-husband's name the other day and warned us he did not need to know you were staying here. I could not believe she did such a thing and challenged her. She got mad with me and said how polite he'd been and how she thought you . . . ' His voice trailed away and he stared down at his shoes.

'Go on, I'm sure it wasn't very flattering but I can take it,' she said rather cynically.

He rested his hand on hers. 'There is no need for me to spell it out. She is not happy about the way things appear to be going between Dante and Alexandra and blames you. Sofia is fiercely protective of her family but

149

sometimes carries it to extremes.'

Marianne moved away slightly, clenched her hands together and took deep breaths to calm down.

'I'm really sorry, my dear. She's gone out this morning to avoid us all; she knows she's in the wrong but it about kills her to admit such a thing. She's a proud woman.'

'I'd better get back to the weeds.' Marianne stood up and tried to smile. 'I want to finish this bed before lunch. Thank you for the lemonade. You'd better go and do what you've been told or you'll be in even more trouble.' It was the closest she could come to being nice and Nico's trace of a smile said he recognized and understood.

'You go ahead. I'll enjoy the air a few more minutes.' He leaned back on the bench.

Too many thoughts swirled around her head to concentrate on the garden but she persevered. Why couldn't Robert let go? Marianne shivered, despite the hot sun.

* ★ *

The house felt empty when she wandered back downstairs after cleaning up for lunch. No doubt Nico was resting and Antonio still worked in the garden but there was no sign of Caterina in the kitchen. The counter was covered in dishes and saucepans sat abandoned on the stove as if she'd been interrupted in the middle of cooking. Marianne picked up a raw carrot and gnawed on it while getting a glass of cold water to drink.

'Trouble. You bring trouble to this house.' Caterina's harsh voice resonated through the silence. The woman stood in the doorway all dressed to go out with her habitual apron replaced by a black shawl.

'I'm sorry — what are you talking about?'

'First you make eyes at Signor Dante, then your husband call and make argument with Signor Nico and Signora Sofia and now you make my niece lose her job and her young man.' Caterina crossed herself and frowned, deepening the lines on her wrinkled face.

Stunned by the vicious attack, Marianne couldn't speak for a minute. 'I'm sorry you feel that way but I can see there's no point trying to explain myself.' She crossed the room to leave but Caterina grabbed her arm, digging in her sharp fingers and stopping her in her tracks.

'You should leave. Go home where you belong.'

'I'll be gone very soon.' Marianne stumbled over her words.

'Go today before you cause any more trouble,' she hissed.

'She is not going anywhere.'

Marianne startled at the sound of Gabe's stern voice.

'Caterina, I suggest you go to see your family now. We will get our own lunch. You've worked for our family a long time, but if you cannot be polite to Signorina Westlake then you can no longer work here. I'm sorry. Think before you return.' His arm slipped around her waist in an obvious gesture of solidarity and for once Marianne didn't consider pushing him away.

'We will see about that, Signor Dante. Your mother will not like to hear what you say to me.' Her threat was clear.

'This is my house, Caterina. It is not up to my mother.'

After the woman left, slamming the door behind her, neither of them spoke for a moment.

'I'm sorry. She had no right to speak to you that way.'

'Maybe not, but she's right isn't she?' Her voice shook with a touch of hysteria. 'I've caused trouble in my own family with my marriage and the ugly divorce and now I'm doing the same thing here.' She rambled on but Gabe pulled her tighter into his embrace and pressed a gentle kiss on her lips.

'Come and sit down.' He eased away and steered her towards one of the kitchen chairs. 'I'm fixing us a drink. I don't know about you but I could do with one.' Gabe opened the nearest cupboard door and took out a bottle and two small glasses, pouring a clear liquid into both.

She obediently took the glass he offered and sipped, nearly choking on the potent liquid. 'What on earth's that?'

'Grappa. You drink whisky while we prefer this.' Gabe drained his in one swallow and reached for the bottle. 'Another?'

Marianne shook her head. 'Goodness, no. I don't need to add drunkard to my list of sins.' Her small laugh and his responding smile made her feel a tiny bit better.

'See, life isn't completely dreadful is it?'

'No, and I'm sorry I overreacted.'

'I don't blame you. This isn't exactly turning out to be the quiet break you'd expected, is it?'

Gabe's ironic words were so accurate she burst into a peal of laughter. 'You could say that. The next time Andy offers to arrange anything for me I believe I'll pass.'

'Really?' He touched her cheek lightly and stared deep into her eyes. 'I'm glad you accepted his offer, trouble or not. I can't imagine my life without you in it now.'

The quiet certainty of his words took her breath away.

'Finally, I've found a way to stop you talking,' he joked.

'You could've chosen something less drastic.' She quickly changed the subject. 'Anyway, tell me about your morning.' She checked her watch. 'I didn't expect you back yet.'

Gabe rubbed at his forehead. 'Andrea Batti arrived to take over the hotel and I needed to get Enrico Galasso back in to show him how some things are run, so you can imagine it was tense. The kitchen's running fairly smoothly and Mario's doing all right so far. I'm not convinced we'll keep him as head chef long term but I'll get Andrea's opinion in a few weeks.'

'What about Florenze? I suppose Caterina heard the news from her family which is why she threw a fit.'

He smiled slightly. 'Yes, but she didn't hear the complete story because the girl accepted my offer so she isn't out of work. She'll stay a year to finish up her classes and get experience alongside Andrea, then hopes to move to Rome. In time she'll be able to help repay her father's debts.'

'I'm so relieved. I felt dreadful she lost her job because of something I did, even if it was partly her own fault. What about Philippe? I assume the engagement's over?'

Gabe nodded and took another sip from his refilled glass. 'Yes, and her family feel bad about pushing her towards him in the first place. Of course the news about the hotel is all around the town because Sicilians love to gossip and everyone knows each other's business over there. Florenze is embarrassed right now but she'll survive. The Galassos aren't happy but they're not my problem anymore.'

'Will you report them to the police?'

His face turned serious. 'I would, but my father says no. He knows what it would do to the family so can't be part of that. If a similar thing happened in one of his other hotels he wouldn't hesitate, but the international business-man disappears when it comes to the Bella Rosa because it was his first hotel. He hates it being tainted by scandal and refuses to make things worse.' Gabe threw up his hands in surrender. 'It's his choice.'

'What about Alexandra?' Marianne was almost afraid to ask. 'I assume lunch got cancelled?'

He grimaced. 'You could say that. She wanted to meet early because she had a job this afternoon and when I arrived said she only wanted a drink after we'd spoken. As you English say, to make a long story short I told her I loved her as a friend but there was something missing, and so I couldn't marry her.'

'Oh, Gabe, how unoriginal to use the old 'I just don't love you that way' line.'

'But it's true,' he protested. 'What else could I say? I wanted to be honest but she didn't appreciate it.' Gabe's hands gesticulated his obvious confusion with the vagaries of women. 'And yes, she did mention you because I know you're wondering.'

'I assume I'm now the Scarlet Woman of Pozzala.' She tried to laugh but didn't do a very good job.

'Something like that.'

He didn't elaborate and Marianne didn't ask any more. She'd had enough slanders on her character today. 'Do your parents know yet?'

He shook his head. 'I'll tell them in a minute but I wanted you to be the first to hear.'

She hesitated, wary of starting the next conversation, but knowing it had to come. 'Your mother's been out all morning. I . . . don't think your parents are speaking to each other.' The expression on Gabe's face hinted at a mixture of worry and anger and his hands tightened so hard on the glass she was surprised it didn't shatter. 'I spoke to your father earlier out in the garden and he explained about last night.' Very calmly she told him everything Nico shared with her and the strain deepened in his eyes. 'I've been thinking and I . . . '

'You are not leaving early so don't consider the idea. We are perfectly able to keep you safe.'

Marianne lowered her gaze. 'You have enough to worry about. If I go home . . . '

'Have you rung Andy or your parents?'

'No,' she whispered, on the verge of tears.

He rubbed his fingers lightly over her chilled skin. 'I'll talk to Andy and see what he thinks, if you want me to.'

'I honestly don't believe Robert's dangerous to me or anyone else. He likes to be in control, always enjoyed

159

making me wonder what he might do. This is all to make me worry.'

Gabe tipped her chin up. 'He's succeeded too, hasn't he?'

She nodded, ashamed and confused of her feelings.

'I'm going to make us some lunch first. It's always best not to make big decisions on an empty stomach.' He smiled and she had to respond. 'How about you go and see if my father's awake; tell him we'll eat in half an hour. We'll sort out everything else after we've eaten my brilliant spaghetti alla Puttanesca with a little garlic, peppers, olives, tomatoes and anchovies, simple and spicy.' Gabe grinned. 'Rather like me. It's great for getting the brain in good working order.'

'It sounds wonderful. I'm glad one of us can cook.' She got up and headed for the door, turning at the last second. 'Thanks. You're a special man.'

His smile made her heart flip with joy. 'That'll do for now in the way of flattery. Off with you.'

Marianne passed on the message to Nico and decided she'd better to go upstairs and tidy her hair. She heard the squeal of tires on the driveway and went over to peek out of the nearest window. Sofia Alessandro stepped out of her shiny red Mercedes sports car, her hair freshly done and dressed in pure white linen. Her demeanor didn't hint at apology or regret. She strode towards the door, the set of her face indicating she was ready for battle.

Marianne sighed out loud. There went any hope of a peaceful lunch.

13

'Caterina,' Sofia shouted out, her arms full of shopping bags.

Marianne stepped forward and pasted on a bright smile. 'Would you like me to take some of those for you?'

'Yes, thank you, but where's Caterina? Is she busy with lunch?' Sofia thrust several heavy bags into her hands as Marianne wondered how to answer the tricky question. Luckily, before she could respond, Gabe appeared with his shirt sleeves rolled up and the tie disposed of, a wooden spoon in one hand.

'I'm cooking today. Caterina had a family problem to see to but I'm sure she'll be back later.'

Marianne was amazed he could sound so normal, but sensed anger under the surface of his calm, smiling face. She didn't look forward to the certain explosion to come when he tackled his parents.

'Oh, right. I'm going to get changed before we eat.' Sofia glanced into the living room. 'Is your father up?'

'Yes, he'll be out soon. Of course he doesn't know you're back.'

The words hung between them all and Marianne held her breath. Only a slight tightening of his mother's glossy red mouth betrayed any hint of emotion.

'I'm sure it'll be a pleasant surprise,' Sofia declared, ignoring Gabe's dry comment.

'No doubt.'

Sofia swiveled around and stalked off towards her bedroom so Marianne dutifully followed with the rest of the morning's haul of shopping. Walking into their room she dropped the bags on the nearest chair, glanced very quickly at the couple now glaring at each other and left. Before she made it back to the kitchen raised voices followed her through the quiet house.

'Started on each other have they?' Gabe commented as he tasted the sauce he was stirring.

'I think so. There was silence when I went in but it didn't last long.'

'Would you mind laying the table? I think we'll eat in here. It'll be easier to clean up if they start throwing stuff.'

'Is that likely?' she asked, horrified. Her own parents never even raised their voices at each other.

'Who knows? It's been done before.' Seemingly unconcerned, he took out a strand of spaghetti and tested it before draining it through a colander and adding it to the sauce. He tossed it all expertly together. 'Of course I'm going to have my say too which might make it more interesting.' Gabe's twist of a smile immediately took away her appetite. 'Come and taste this. Tell me if it needs more oregano.' He held out a spoon.

Marianne swallowed and burst into a spontaneous smile. 'Oh goodness, that's delicious. I'd say it's perfect, but I'm no cook.'

'If it makes you happy there can't be much wrong with it. I know it's bad manners but I'm going to dish ours up. We'll try to enjoy it before they spoil things.' Gabe gestured towards the table. 'Pour the wine and I'll join you.' He placed a bowl of steaming pasta in front of her, sprinkled it with chopped parsley and grated fresh Parmesan cheese all over the top. 'Eat up.'

They made it about halfway through before Sofia swept into the room followed by Nico, laboring on his crutches. Gabe's hand on her arm kept her in her seat.

'You carry on and I'll see to them,' he whispered. 'Mamma, Papa, sit down and I'll bring the food over. Are you having wine?'

'Not for your father, he's on strong pain medicine,' Sofia snapped.

'I can answer for myself. I broke my leg not my tongue,' he retorted.

'And don't we all know it. If you

hadn't tried to behave like a sixteen-year-old instead of a grown man of nearly sixty we'd be enjoying the sights of Athens today.'

Gabe banged his hand on the table. 'Stop it now. The meal will be ruined if you shout through it. Eat first, then you can carry on your fight.'

He turned around to get their lunch and Marianne noticed how stiffly he held himself. She couldn't think what to do except pour water into Nico's glass, despite the screwed-up disapproval on his face. She allowed Sofia to fill her own with a generous measure of the local red wine. For a meal in the Alessandro house this was ominously quiet, the only comments being polite ones about the food and the pleasant weather.

'How about coffee on the terrace?' Gabe offered and there was muted agreement. 'Marianne, would you mind helping me?'

She swiftly agreed and left Sofia to help Nico.

'If you want to leave us to it I wouldn't blame you.' Gabe threw out the suggestion but she shook her head.

'Not unless you'd prefer it?'

'Not at all. Apart from anything else you might stop me strangling my mother.' The smile didn't reach his black brooding eyes.

'Glad to be of use.' She popped a light kiss on his cheek and picked up the dish of torroncini, the locally made chocolate-covered nougat she'd fallen in love with, ready to head outside.

* * *

Putting down his empty coffee cup Gabe rested his large hands on the table. 'Right, Mamma, I'd like an explanation.'

'What for?' Sofia blustered, smoothing her hair back into its already perfect style.

'Why you told Marianne's ex-husband she was here after I specifically asked you not to?'

The thread of steel running through his voice made Marianne quail, as did the stillness of his usually expressive hands.

Sofia's beautiful features twisted with fury as she turned on him. 'You are a stupid boy, Dante Gabriele Alessandro. Don't you see what she's done?' The glance she threw in Marianne's direction could've seared raw steak to a crisp. 'She couldn't hold on to her own husband so she's digging her claws into you instead. Soon she'll go home and you'll be left with nothing. Alexandra's a proud woman and will not come running back if you continue to treat her badly.'

'Leave her out of this for a minute, please. Right now all I want to know is why you told Robert Blackwell Marianne is here. It's a very simple question.'

Sofia played with her torroncini wrapper before looking back up at her son and for the first time there was a touch of regret in her expressive eyes.

'Maybe I was hasty. I thought if Marianne left things might get back to normal.' She shrugged. 'I'm sorry. It was reckless of me and if I've caused any trouble . . . ' Her words ebbed away and she dropped her gaze down to the table.

Nico reached over and took hold of her hand. 'You have, *tesoro*, my love, but hopefully we can all make the rest of Marianne's stay pleasant and safe.' When his wife only nodded briefly he carried on. 'Dante, why don't you tell us how your lunch went so we get all of this out of the way?'

There was a heavy pause as Gabe took another sip of espresso then put down the small cup, glancing at Marianne before starting to speak. 'We obviously didn't end up eating lunch or I wouldn't be here, which should give you a clue. I told her the truth. I value her dearly as a friend, but my feelings aren't enough for marriage and I'd be doing her a disservice to pretend otherwise.'

'Oh, Dante, how could you speak to her that way after all these years?' Sadness ran through his mother's voice.

'I had to. It wasn't easy but I couldn't let this go on any longer.'

The finality in his tone convinced Marianne he meant every word.

'I know I'm not supposed to say this,' Sofia hesitated, 'but has this anything to do with Marianne?'

She held her breath, hoping he wouldn't say anything hard to take back later.

'Yes and no. I should've been honest with Alexandra long before now but I was a coward and let it drift on because I didn't want to hurt her or you both. Meeting Marianna has changed things for me but . . . before she protests I must say I completely understand she's not ready for another relationship. There may never be a time when it is right for us but I'm prepared to wait and hope.'

His warm smile, full of something she was very afraid was love, pierced her heart and cracked another of the walls she'd erected for self-preservation. Gabe laid his hand gently on hers. 'I'm not asking for anything, Marianna. I will be whatever you need for now and maybe one day things will be different.'

She couldn't answer beyond a half-smile and slight shrug. It wasn't a conversation to have today and especially not in front of his parents.

'I don't know about anyone else but my leg is telling me it's time for another stupid rest.' Nico glanced tenderly at his wife. 'Will you join me?'

'Of course, you silly man, or you'll probably fall off your crutches.' The softening in every plane of Sofia's face made her meaning clear, even if her words were less than loving.

Gabe and Marianne watched them go, bickering as they went, and shared a conspiratorial smile.

'It is their way and always has been. Fire or ice, with very little in between.' His slow smile sent her pulse soaring. 'I couldn't handle it myself. I crave someone more even-keeled and straightforward so I know where I stand.'

She flushed at the obvious implication and searched for a reply, but while she was still thinking he cradled her face and kissed her. 'I won't apologize, even if I should. It's a kiss. Nothing more and nothing less. It's not a lifetime promise but an expression of how you make me feel.'

Gabe's challenging words made her smile. 'Every time I'm sure I can resist your charm I'm proved wrong.' Her voice faltered. 'But you're right when you say I'm not ready. I can't trust my judgment at the moment and don't know when or if I ever will again. I fell for another charming, good-looking man who promised me his unending love but changed into someone I didn't recognize. Do you blame me for being wary a second time?'

'Not at all.' He picked up her hand and pressed a gentle kiss on her palm.

'Let's concentrate on having an enjoyable couple of weeks and I promise not to pressure you into anything beyond friendship.'

When the simple touch of his hand sent her in to such turmoil the idea of being 'friends' with Gabe sounded impossible, but she wanted to try. 'Let's see how it goes.' Marianne picked up and unwrapped another of the delicious sweets. 'What's your plan for the rest of the day?'

'I'm afraid I need to work. Having to sort out the hotel and now deal with Papa's accident has put me way behind.'

'Sorry, and I'm sure I'm holding you up too. I don't want you to feel a need to babysit me. I'll do the things I promised to be careful but you don't have to watch over me every minute.'

'Don't say that again. Your being here is a pleasure for me, plus I don't break promises to old friends. Andy asked me to provide you a safe haven, which is what I plan to do.' The smile hovering

173

around his mouth softened the rather severe words.

'Thank you.' She glanced around the table. 'I'll clear up lunch.'

'That'd be a great help. I must go and make some phone calls. I'll be in my study if you need me. And remember . . . '

'Don't worry, if I go out I'll tell someone and I'll take my phone with me. I'm probably going to stay around here anyway and enjoy a lazy afternoon after being out in the garden working this morning.'

'All right, I know when I'm beaten.' He threw up his hands in surrender. 'I'll see you later.'

Left on her own she didn't rush to make a start, merely enjoyed the warm sun and the scent drifting across from the exotic purple bougainvillea plants. Antonio had tried to explain the actual flowers in the center were small and it was the brightly colored leaf bracts surrounding them which drew the eye. All of a sudden the insistent sound of the buzzer from the front gate disturbed her musing.

Marianne ran inside and tried to answer as best she could but could only make out a garbled voice saying something about flowers. She pushed the button to open the gate and went to stand outside, waiting for the visitor to enter. A young Italian carrying a large wrapped bouquet of flowers walked down the driveway and thrust them into her arms. She tried to ask if they were for Signora Alessandro, that would probably be a typical Nico gesture after an argument, but he insisted they were for Signorina Westlake. Not about to stand there arguing she thanked him and went back indoors.

She took them into the kitchen and began to unwrap the plastic. Yellow roses. Marianne gasped and slapped her hand across her mouth to stop from crying out. There was no card but she didn't need one. The first time Robert brought her flowers he'd said one of the meanings of the yellow rose was

'Remember Me' which was what he always expected her to do.

She sank into a chair and large tears dripped down her face as the flowers fell from her hands onto the floor. Would she never be free?

14

'Signorina, what is wrong?'

Through a glaze of tears Marianne looked up at Caterina standing in front of her. 'I didn't hear you come in.'

'No, but I hear you.'

An awkward silence filled the room and Marianne guessed the other woman was remembering, as she was, their earlier conversation.

'I wanted to see you and say I am sorry. My niece told me off. She say you were kind to her and that she did wrong. Because you speak to Signor Dante she get better job now.'

She picked her words carefully. 'Florenze is a good girl and I wanted to help her if I could. Is her family very upset?'

Caterina nodded. 'Yes, but not at you or Signor Dante. They angry because they not realize the Galassos are bad people. Enrico Galasso was a wicked boy in school when we were children together, and Philippe is like his father.'

Marianne managed a slight smile. 'I'm glad it's worked out all right and I know Signor Dante will be pleased to see you back. He's working in his study at the moment. Oh, and Signor Nico and Signora Sofia are fine now.' She didn't add anything about Alexandra because it wasn't her story to tell.

'That is good.' The woman smiled and every line on her darkly tanned face creased into even deeper furrows. 'They always argue and fight then love again. It is their way.' Caterina looked around her domain and shook her head at the mess. 'Signor Dante has been cooking?'

She blushed. 'Yes, but I promised him I'd clear up then I got ... distracted.'

Caterina began to pick up roses from the floor.

'You don't need to do that.' Marianne jumped up and helped to sweep the flowers into a pile on the table. Roughly she wrapped the paper around them and shoved the whole package into the bin. Only when she saw the puzzled expression on the other woman's face did she stop to think how this must look. Women didn't usually throw away beautiful bouquets of roses. 'I didn't want them.' Her voice cracked and Caterina patted her hand.

'They are from the man who hurt you?'

She could only manage a slight nod in case she burst into tears again.

'If he dare come here we send him away and he never come back.'

Her fierce tone made Marianne smile. 'Thank you.'

'I forgot my . . . ' Gabe's voice trailed away as he looked at them both. 'Caterina, it's good to see you back.'

A long stream of rapid Italian poured from the older woman.

'It'll be all right. Mamma and Papa only know you had a family problem to sort. There is no need for any more to be said.'

'Thank you, Signor Dante. I would not want them thinking Caterina is crazy old lady.'

Gabe hugged her and the cook's face flushed a deep dark crimson. After he let go his attention fixed on Marianne, sizing her up with his piercing dark eyes. 'What's wrong?' His gaze darted around the room and lit on the flowers sticking out of the rubbish.

'You two go outside and talk,' Caterina interrupted. 'I need to clean up before your mother come in and call me a lazy woman.'

Marianne thanked her and was gently shooed from the kitchen along with Gabe.

'What did you come in for anyway?' she asked, wanting to put off yet another discussion about her ex-husband.

'Uh, just my favorite pen; I'd left it by the kitchen phone earlier. That's not important now. What's going on?'

'Some flowers were delivered to me.'

'Is that a problem? From my experience women usually enjoy getting flowers. Is it because you don't like yellow roses or because of who sent them?' He scrutinized her some more. 'I'd bet a large sum it's the latter.'

'You're right,' Marianne sighed, 'although he's made me hate yellow roses too, but that's incidental.'

'Do you want to tell me what the message said?'

'There wasn't one, but there didn't need to be. The very first time he bought me yellow roses Robert told me they meant 'Remember Me'. He's telling me I will never be free of him.' She heard the edge of hysteria in her voice but when Gabe wrapped his warm arms around her a calm sensation trickled through her blood.

'Only if you let him. I have a plan. Later we will go for a run and then I'm taking you out to dinner. We will show him you are not afraid.'

'But you're busy,' she protested.

'I will never be too busy for you. One

day you will understand, Marianna. Now go and help Caterina in the kitchen. You need something to occupy yourself and it will help her out too.'

'I'll be happy to. She was so kind when she returned and found me here upset. We are all right now. I didn't mention Alexandra — that's your job.'

He smiled at her bossiness. 'Yes, Signorina, I will talk to her later. Right now I'm going back to work and you will stay busy until I am free.'

She agreed without an argument.

* * *

Despite Gabe's longer legs Marianne managed to keep up as they made their way up the mountain before angling back down and around Pozzala, slowing a little through the town, and picking up the pace again as they headed towards home.

They fast-walked the last few hundred meters to begin their cool down and her breathing eased enough to allow for conversation again. 'You're not too slow for an old man,' she jested.

'Thanks, Squib.' He poked her arm. 'You don't do too badly for a short thing either.'

Punching in the gate code he let them back in and they spent a couple of minutes stretching. As she reached for the door knob he stopped her and swung her around to face him. Gabe trailed his finger down her face and lingered on her shoulder.

'Gabe,' she gasped.

'Sorry.' He jerked away, his face suddenly dark and serious. 'Let's go in. We need a drink.'

Gabe strode away before she could answer, which was just as well because she didn't have any words to express her confusion. In the kitchen he passed her a large glass of iced water before standing at the opposite end of the counter.

'Maybe we should stay in for dinner,' she said flatly.

'If you prefer.' Gabe's clipped tone

suggested he was struggling too. 'I'm going to shower, unless you want the bathroom first?'

'No, please go ahead.' The politeness between them hurt, but might be the only way for them to survive. The last thing she wanted was to hurt him. Tears pressed at the back of her eyes but she refused to let them out. Perhaps she should change her ticket and go home early?

'Ah, Dante, my boy, I was looking for you. Signor Beppo called from the Vincenzo Bellini.' Nico hobbled into the room followed closely by Sofia. 'There are problems with the renovations — the decorators are going wildly over budget and apparently the carpet's not the one we chose. He wanted me to come and sort it out but I explained my situation.' He gestured towards his leg. 'Is there any chance you could go to Rome for a few days?'

'Of course, but will you be all right?'

'I'm not exactly short of nursemaids, am I?' Nico chuckled, but all of a sudden he stopped. 'I appreciate how hard you work. I know the hotel business is not what you'd planned for your life but you do an excellent job.'

She'd never heard anyone mention anything on those lines before and held her breath. Gabe's features betrayed little apart from a slight tightening around his jaw and the way his hands hung motionless by his side.

'Thank you, Papa. I always try to do my best. If you'll excuse me I need to go and pack and make some arrangements.' Without waiting for an answer he stood, kissed his mother's cheek and nodded slightly at his father and Marianne before leaving the kitchen.

For a moment no one spoke.

Marianne took a deep swallow of water to clear her dry throat, deciding to ask the question burning her mind. 'What did he originally want to do anyway? I do remember him being an excellent painter when we first met.' He would hate to hear her asking these questions but if he was here she would be keeping her mouth shut.

'Dante was always a creative boy.' Sofia's unusually soft voice almost sounded sad. 'He understands our business is a huge job and he's expected to carry it on.' She gave her husband a wistful look. 'We had hoped for many children, but it was not to be and so everything fell to him. Sometimes I feel guilty.'

Nico picked up her hand and kissed it. 'Don't. He has a good life and I believe he's happy enough. Many young men would envy his good fortune.'

Marianne thought of the satisfaction she got from teaching and wondered if Gabe felt the same about his job. An expensive sports car, a beautiful house, designer clothes, and the money to indulge in all the high-risk sports he loved were all very well, but in the end might not give him lasting happiness. She needed to remember she was a guest and it wasn't her place to interfere.

'He is a grown man and if he wants

to change things he must speak up,' Nico said decisively. 'Now, I would like to take you two lovely ladies out into the garden. Antonio told me the new Bird of Paradise plants are in flower and worth seeing. There's enough shade now we won't be too hot.'

The discussion was obviously at an end and the glances between Gabe's parents told Marianne they'd teamed back up. Plainly they weren't going to talk about personal family matters in front of her any more today. She conceded with a polite smile and opened the door leading to the patio, holding it back for Nico to hobble through. The next hour passed pleasantly as they sat on the bench and he launched into a commentary on the garden, giving more horticultural details than she or Sofia needed.

Out of the blue Gabe appeared, freshly dressed in dark trousers and a smart blue and white striped shirt, carrying a large wood tray. 'Caterina insists you will all drop dead of exhaustion if you don't have a cold drink and some of her famous almond biscuits.'

Marianne moved to give him room to sit and smelled the fresh lime soap he'd showered with, noticing the damp hair clinging to his neck and curling slightly at the ends. She gulped down the cold lemonade in an effort to cool her flushed skin.

'I had a great idea while I was upstairs and it's all arranged if Marianna agrees.' There was an unmistakable challenge in his voice. 'She's never been to Rome so why don't I take her with me?'

Three days alone with him — she didn't think so. Before she could put a stop to his ridiculous idea Sofia jumped right in.

'What a wonderful idea. I don't know why we didn't think of it first.' She leant across and squeezed Marianne's arm. 'My youngest sister, Angelina, is in charge of public relations for the hotel and lives in the owner's suite on the top floor. She's always happy when any of the family are there and there are several extra bedrooms so it won't be a problem. It's the perfect opportunity for you to see our beautiful capital city. Of course August isn't ideal — it's very hot and many of the shops and restaurants close for the owners to take their own holidays, but on the other hand it's not so crowded.'

Marianne gave a weak smile. 'Well, I'm not sure.'

'No more arguments, my dear,' Nico interrupted. 'This pesky ex-husband of yours will think you're still here and we've got Antonio and Caterina to care for us. Rome is such a beautiful city. You'll have plenty of opportunity to see all the great sights while this poor man works.' He slapped his son's shoulder. 'Well done, my boy for thinking of that. You'll take the jet of course.'

'It's all arranged. We should be back by Friday.'

Marianne gave up trying to say

anything else. They'd plainly all decided for her.

'You might want to get some things sorted before dinner as we'll leave early in the morning. You've got time to do laundry if necessary.' Gabe grinned and she gave in and smiled back, her excitement at the prospect of seeing Rome overcoming the nagging feeling this wasn't a wise trip to make.

15

Marianne peered out of the limousine's concealing black glass as they drove slowly down the winding roads towards the Catania airport. It struck her as incongruous to be in this luxurious car but driving past mountains of rubbish by the side of the road and half-completed buildings abandoned in the middle of construction. She glanced over at Gabe but he was intent on checking phone calls and emails on his phone. Today he was in complete business mode with his sleek dark suit, silk tie, handmade shoes and dark sunglasses — handsome, suave and very remote. They'd barely exchanged a word so far but she knew by now he wasn't much of a morning person.

Last night she'd briefly tried to suggest it'd be better if she didn't come to Rome with him but he'd devastated her feeble arguments in an instant. 'I told Andy I'd watch out for you, which I can't do if you're here and I'm in Rome.' She'd attempted to ask if he intended to keep her prisoner while he worked but he'd raised one eyebrow and told her not to be silly. She could go where she wanted as long as his appointed escort went too. Marianne slammed her lips shut and gave in.

A gleaming white plane complete with the red and gold Alessandro Hotels logo waited for them on the tarmac and the car pulled up right by the steps.

'Leave the bags. Luca will see to them.' Gabe leapt out of the car and briskly walked around to open her door from out of the chauffeur's hands.

She stepped out and smoothed down her dress before walking quickly up the airplane steps.

'I suggest you sit on the right hand side of the plane so you'll see the approach to Rome better when we arrive. It's only about a seventy-five minute journey. I hope you don't mind but I've got work to do. Tell the crew if you need anything.' Gabe made himself comfortable and got out a sheaf of papers to read and his laptop ready for after takeoff.

Settling into the spacious leather seat Marianne decided to enjoy the moment. This was something to tell her family about when she went home. They weren't familiar with the world of chauffeured cars and private planes, but she had to admit it'd be easy to get used to. Her pupils would laugh to see her now, minus the sweatsuits and trainers she normally lived in. She hadn't wanted to let Gabe down and chose to put on a new slim-fitting yellow linen shift dress, setting off her freshly acquired tan. She'd even managed to find some make-up and fuss a little more with her hair, longer now and shining with natural highlights from the sun. A new pair of gold sandals finished the look and she wasn't unpleased with the effect. Judging by the way Gabe's eyes widened when she came down to breakfast he wasn't either, although how she felt about that she wasn't sure.

For most of the flight she chatted to the flight attendant, indulging in a glass of champagne while they swapped life stories.

'We're approaching Rome. If you care to look I'll point out some of the sights.' Gabe slipped into the seat next to her and leaned across. 'There's the Tiber River.' She tried to concentrate on where his hand pointed, rather than his disconcerting nearness. 'That's the Olympic Stadium and over there's the Castel Sant' Angelo. It was built by Hadrian as a mausoleum and went through many changes, ending up as a museum.' Gabe dropped his hand to rest it on her knee but lifted it away as he pointed again. 'St. Peter's is coming up and there's the Vatican.'

'This is amazing. I can't believe I'm seeing all these places I've only ever heard of.'

'Are you glad I brought you?'

'Definitely.'

'Look quickly, there's the Colosseum.'

She couldn't take her gaze away and craned her neck until the magnificent ruins disappeared from sight.

'We're coming in to land. See how we're paralleling the old Appian Way.' Gabe pointed to a tree-lined road running alongside their descent.

As the wheels touched down he took her hand and kissed it, glancing back up to fix her with his warm dark eyes. 'Welcome to Roma, *sei cosi bella*, my beautiful one.'

★ ★ ★

Another black limousine whisked them into the center of the city. She wanted to take it all in but saw most of it through the gaps in her fingers, shoved up in front of her eyes to lessen the impact. If this was a less crowded time to come she wouldn't like to see it busy.

Italian drivers appeared to totally disregard the rules of the road and to survive it was necessary to do the same, which did nothing good for her blood pressure. Their chauffeur Francesco wove through traffic with an ease hinting at years of practice.

'Look up the next street on our left and you'll see the Trevi Fountain.' Gabe prodded her arm. 'You'll find it easier to spot it if you put your hands down.' His good-humored words made her blush and she tried to appear as if this wasn't frightening her half to death. He wrapped an arm around her shoulders and whispered in her ear. 'Next time we'll bring my car and I'll show you how to really do this.'

'Is that a threat or a promise?' she teased.

'Which would you like it to be?'

It took all her self-discipline to look away and murmur something incomprehensible in reply. Gabe didn't say another word until they pulled into a square of elegant old buildings and pointed to the large ornate front of one large structure, framed with the now-familiar red and gold Alessandro flags.

'This is the Vincenzo Bellini hotel. Don't worry, we have reserved parking around the back.'

Marianne was in a whirl as they entered the stunning lobby with its marble floors and exquisite glittering chandeliers. Gabe was greeted with typical Italian effusiveness by the manager and they were taken in a private lift, complete with extravagant gilt framed mirrors, up to the top floor.

'My aunt will join us soon. Your bedroom is next to Zia Angelina's and mine and the other guest room are on the other side of the shared living room, so we won't have to fight over who has the most space.'

'That sounds wonderful,' she murmured and stared around, overawed by the high, ornately decorated ceilings, beautiful antique furniture of a size that'd never fit into any typical English hotel room, elaborate wallpaper and more crystal chandeliers. 'Modest isn't it?' Marianne joked, catching his immediate smile.

'A little fussy for your taste?'

'Maybe for yours too?'

'Yes. When we bought this place I wanted to modernize it some, not by ruining the old architecture but blending it with some newer designs. My father refused and said this was what our guests expected.'

She wasn't sure how much more to ask. 'Is business good?'

'It could be better. We're starting to get a few negative comments from business people wanting internet connections and more efficient showers. Father says they can go to one of the modern hotels if they want those things, but I keep arguing we need to adapt.' He shrugged.

'I'm guessing it's the perennial problem with a family business.' Marianne chose her words carefully. 'If you weren't related you could be more honest and resign if you really couldn't compromise. It's harder when it's your name over the door.'

For a second he seemed about to say something but the shutters came down and Gabe slid back into charming host mode. 'Enough of my problems. Let's not spoil the day. Lunch should arrive in a few minutes if you'd care to freshen up first. I'll show you to your room.'

'Thank you.' What else could she say?

Over fried calamari and veal Milanese they kept the conversation light. He told her about his favorite places to go in the city and promised to spend time with her when he wasn't busy. As they sipped their coffee there was a knock on the door and Gabe called out in Italian.

Marianne couldn't stop staring as a man entered. By any standards Gabe wasn't a small man, but the newcomer topped him by a good six inches and his massive, heavily muscled body bulged out of a black suit straining at the seams. Mirrored sunglasses, a white shirt and narrow black tie completed the look — one straight out of Mafia movie casting.

'Marianna, I'd like you to meet my old friend Carlo Lucci. He's going to show you around Rome when I'm working.'

She struggled to keep a straight face and thanked him.

'It will be my pleasure.' Carlo gave a slight bow. 'Rome is the most beautiful city in the world and I love nothing better than showing her off.' His almost unaccented English surprised her and a touch of humor pulled at the edges of his mouth as he recognized how she'd stereotyped him on sight.

Gabe rattled on in Italian for a few minutes, no doubt giving instructions he didn't want her to understand. Being protected this way rankled, but she bit her lip and said nothing. He turned back to her. 'You must excuse me now. Sit a while and talk with Carlo about what you want to see while we're here. I've asked him to have you back here by eight and we'll dine with my aunt tonight.' He slipped his jacket back on, quickly checked his hair in the mirror, readjusted his tie and left.

Dealing with a bodyguard/tour guide wasn't in her usual day-to-day life and she wasn't quite sure how to behave, but half an hour later she'd forgotten all her qualms. Carlo was a scholar of Italian history, an architecture nut and an unexpectedly amusing man with a dry sense of humor. She could see why he and Gabe were friends.

Deciding to concentrate on the area closest to the hotel today they headed first towards the Quirinale, admiring the exterior of the stunning President's residence before wandering a few more narrow streets to the Trevi Fountain.

'This is the largest Baroque fountain in Italy. That's Oceanus in the chariot drawn by two seahorses and two tritons,' Carlo informed her as they walked all around the elaborate fountain. 'Of course you have to throw in a coin to guarantee your return to the Eternal City.' He smiled, a gesture with a rather menacing touch due to his large number of gold teeth. 'Of course your coin might be stolen by the devils who have nothing better to do than take from the poor, but what can you do?'

Marianne laughed and threw one in anyway, not wanting to take a chance.

'Your feet are good for walking all the way to the Piazza di Spagna?'

'Of course. Is there something special there?'

'That's where you'll find the famous Spanish Steps. Everyone has to walk up the Scalinata, it's the widest staircase in Europe and always covered in tourists and swarming with pickpockets.' He gave an easy shrug. 'We'll stop there for a cold drink. You might like to see Keats's house as well. It's in the same square because most of the Romance poets lived around there.'

Later, tired but content, they sat under the shade of an orange tree in a quiet corner café. Carlo knew the owner and picked the best spot to see the rest of the square so she could people-watch.

'Signorina. This is for you from a friend.'

Marianne startled as a small scruffy boy thrust a paper wrapped package at her but Carlo immediately snatched it away, glared and seized a tight hold of the child's arm. He spoke quickly, the dark angry tone making it clear he wasn't pleased with the interloper's replies.

'What is it? What's wrong?' she asked, but he continued to interrogate before pushing the child away with a clear admonition not to return. 'Carlo, I want to see what is in the package and then I expect you to tell me everything the boy said.'

'Dante told me you are a stubborn woman and he is right.'

'Fine, I'm stubborn, now give it to me.'

He held her away. 'Not until I've checked it out.' Carlo eased back the shiny green paper.

'Oh no. Not here. It can't be.' Marianne stared in horror at the single yellow rose.

16

'Don't react. Turn towards me and take a sip of your drink. Now give me a big smile.'

Marianne followed Carlo's instructions and tried to ignore the waves of nausea spreading through her whole body. All she wanted was to run back to the hotel and lock herself in the room.

'Good girl. Now I'm going to tell you an interesting story and you'll laugh and pretend to tease me as though I'm the most fascinating man on earth.'

'Are you telling me to flirt with you?'

Carlo removed his sunglasses and grinned. 'Precisely.'

She sucked in a deep breath and tried to do as he'd asked. 'You do have very compelling eyes. They're sort of an electric blue. Aren't they rather unusual for an Italian?'

'See, you're doing great. Would it

surprise you to learn my mother was Danish? She's to blame for the eyes and they're one reason I wear sunglasses most of the time. Blue eyes aren't intimidating.' The aforementioned eyes twinkled with mischief.

'Can you explain what we're doing? What's the point of all this?' she murmured while attempting to keep up the flirtatious smile.

He lowered his head, bending over her hand and touching it gently. 'This Robert Blackwell doesn't know Dante, does he?'

'No, he wasn't around when Andy brought him from university to visit.'

'Good, although we mustn't assume he hasn't seen a picture. If I'm correct he's assuming I'm Dante. If that's not the case he's wondering who the other man is you're out with. Either one should annoy him which is fine by me.'

Marianne jerked to glance back around but Carlo placed his hand firmly on hers and forced her to stay still.

'Remember what we're doing,' he warned.

'Sorry, but the idea he's watching gives me the creeps.'

'I'm pretty certain he is. He set up the boy to see your reaction and we're not going to give him the satisfaction of being proved right. If I'd been more on the ball I wouldn't have got angry with the boy, but I can't take it back now. Your ex can think I'm overprotective and jealous.'

'What do we do now?'

'We're going to carry on as if nothing important happened. You're a woman so we're going to wander along the Via Veneto and look at all the wonderful fashion and jewelry shops. Only after we've done that at a leisurely pace, making it clear we're . . . together, then we'll we return to the hotel.' A touch of color tinged his dark olive skin.

'What do you mean?'

'Well, if it's not too offensive I'll hold your hand and look . . . interested, shall we say?'

For a brief moment she wondered what the sensitive and cultured Robert would think seeing her 'with' this giant of a man. She wanted to get this over with and make it clear to Robert he was wasting his time. 'I'm game if you think it'll help.' Deciding to go all in she reached over to touch his face and pressed a soft kiss on his cheek. Carlo almost choked and quickly covered it with a cough.

'Dante's got his hands full with you, hasn't he?' he teased.

'He hasn't 'got' me at all,' Marianne instantly retorted. 'We're good friends and that's it. I'm not looking for a relationship with anyone right now.'

Carlo nodded although he didn't look very convinced. Nobody seemed to believe her.

★ ★ ★

The late afternoon sun softened the room and took away some of the formality, allowing Marianne to feel more comfortable in the luxurious hotel. She'd finally convinced Carlo to leave by promising not to open the door to anyone apart from Gabe. Wandering over to look out of the window, she contemplated sitting on the balcony but decided it might not fall into the category of being careful.

Against her will she thought of Robert and how he'd once been — handsome, well-educated and with a great sense of humor. It'd been easy for her to ignore the flashes of temper he'd shown with other people because with her he'd always been kind and thoughtful. But the minute they were married he'd changed. She'd always been a strong, independent woman but over the next year he'd eroded away at her self-esteem until she'd had no choice but to leave him. Marianne guessed she might never understand why it'd happened and accepting that was hard.

What she needed now was her favorite method of relaxation — a long, hot, perfumed bath. Soon she lay back in the wonderful deep claw-footed tub, her head resting on the soft pillow provided, and simply wallowed. Marianne had a weakness for complimentary toiletries in all hotels, but this one took it to a new level. Everything she could imagine was available and all in wonderful matching scents and of the finest quality. She'd make the most of every single one and hopefully afterwards she'd be calmer about the evening ahead.

Marianne almost dozed in the candlelight — if they thoughtfully provided candles she considered it her duty to use them — and she sipped a glass of sparkling water, totally relaxed.

'Marianna, Marianna, where are you?'

Gabe's distraught voice disturbed her, followed up by a string of Italian curses and the sound of doors banging. Reluctantly she pulled up slightly out of the froth of lily-scented bubbles. 'I'm in the bath. Stop shouting.' Suddenly the bathroom door started to open and she yelled, 'Stay out. What on earth do you think you're doing?' The door closed and she sunk back into the water.

'I could ask the same of you,' Gabe called in through.

'Uh, I'm taking a bath, what do you think I'm doing?'

'Carlo told you to stay . . . '

'Dante Gabriele Alessandro, he told me to stay in the suite and the last time I checked that included the bathroom. He didn't say I had to remain in the same chair and not move until you deigned to appear.'

'Maybe I overreacted. I'm sorry. It worried me when he brought me up to date with what happened this afternoon.'

'Would you mind if we finish this conversation after I'm dressed? I'm getting cold.'

'Sorry.'

She felt his embarrassment through the closed door. 'I'll join you when I'm decent. If you wouldn't mind ordering some tea I'd appreciate that too.'

Taking her time she dried off, slathered herself with richly scented lotion, and then slipped into one of the thick toweling bathrobes provided for guests. First stop would have to be the bedroom for her clothes because no way was she sitting and talking to Gabe without being properly dressed.

The second she walked into the living room Gabe stood and gestured for her to join him on the plush red velvet sofa.

'Would you care to pour? I'm sure I'd do it wrong,' he said, with little of his usual confidence.

A loaded tea tray sat on the ornate low table in front of them. She fought to keep her hands steady as she picked up the fine china teapot and poured out two cups of steaming-hot tea. Marianne helped herself to a crisp chocolate biscuit, more to have something to do with her hands than because she was hungry.

'I want to apologize again for . . . almost bursting in on you. It's just . . . '

He pushed his fingers through his hair, plainly agitated. 'I couldn't see you anywhere.'

She touched his hand. 'It's all right. I'm sorry you were worried.'

'Let's forget it. Why don't you tell me all about your day, and not just the unpleasant part?'

'It was wonderful up until then. Carlo's very good company.'

'Not too good I hope or I'll be jealous,' he joked. Gabe took a sip of tea and grimaced. 'God, I don't know how you can drink this stuff. It's tasteless.'

'Just because you poison your insides with dark sludge at regular intervals. This is far healthier.' She'd never learn to like espresso as long as she lived.

He smirked. 'We'll have to agree to disagree on that. Carry on with your story.'

She did and they smiled together, talking about all the places she and Carlo walked to and how, on the whole, she'd had a much better day than Gabe.

'I was so frustrated I nearly bashed the chief decorator's and manager's heads together. In the end I had to get tough and set strict budget guidelines and pretty much tell the manager to stay out of it.'

'Was the carpet truly awful?'

He winced. 'Worse than awful. We'd selected a tasteful pale green and for some bizarre reason he'd changed it to a neon lime-green. I suspect he'd been bribed to buy it from an unscrupulous dealer. I told him it'd better be removed by tomorrow morning or he's fired. The other should be installed by Friday morning so I plan to see it down before we leave.'

'Do you spend a lot of time on similar problems?'

He frowned. 'Not quite as much these days. I do more of the initial negotiations and financing.'

'Presumably it involves a lot of traveling. Don't you get tired of it?'

A strange look crossed Gabe's face and he put the cup down, tugged at his tie and quickly removed it and his jacket. 'Yes,' he snapped.

'I'm curious. What would you prefer to do if you had the choice?'

He shook his head and gave her a wry smile. 'Marianna, get rid of the notion I could've been the next Michelangelo. Yes, I was a decent painter but making my living from it would never have happened. I don't hate the hotel business, in fact I enjoy many aspects of it. What I really dislike, which is a feeble complaint to make, is we've become too big, too successful. If I had my choice I'd sell the business and maybe start a very small chain of boutique hotels or perhaps something to cater for more adventurous travelers.'

'Have you ever mentioned this to your father?'

'You're persistent aren't you? No, I haven't because Alessandro Hotels is his baby and he gets a real kick out of its growth. He'd consider my ideas a step back.'

'I think he'd respect you being honest. What've you got to lose?'

Gabe rested his hand gently against the side of her face and she unconsciously leaned into his touch. 'I know you're right. It's rather like the situation with Alexandra where it was easier to drift along than upset everyone. I suppose it doesn't show me in a very good light.'

'I can hardly call you a coward when I'm pretty much here because I ran away from my life, now can I?'

He looked dubious. 'It's a different thing.'

'Yes, but I've got to make up my mind to return. School starts in another three weeks and they've offered me my job back. I need to move out and find somewhere to live. My parents are happy for me to stay, but at twenty-five that's not what I need.'

'Changing the subject slightly,' he said, 'I've been wondering off and on all day how Robert knows we're here. Somebody close to my family must be in contact with him but I can't imagine who.'

The same thought had bothered her from the moment the boy placed the yellow rose in her hand. 'I don't know. The only person I told was Andy and there's no way he's responsible.'

'I asked my father and he got rather uptight. He's very defensive after Mamma's mistake over the phone call. Caterina's the only other person who knows you're here and I can hardly see her willingly telling some strange Englishman anything.'

Marianne felt awful. 'I'm sorry to cause all this trouble.'

He seized her hands. 'Don't you dare start that again. Now we're going to forget him and enjoy the evening. My aunt Angelina has a prior dinner engagement but she'll be here later. I'm going to take you over to Trastevere. It's my favorite section of Rome, although it's across the Tiber River so many people say it's not really part of the city.'

'I'll go and change.' Gabe's dark eyes rested on her and Marianne felt pleasantly aware of herself as a woman again.

'You're perfect as you are.' He cleared his throat. 'The dress suits you.'

'It's old, but I've got a couple of smarter ones with me.' She glanced down at the simple pink linen shift, certain it wasn't the right thing for a classy Italian night out.

'Trust me. We're going to my favorite pizza place so you don't need anything fancier.' His hand trailed down her bare arm lingering for a moment on the racing pulse at her wrist. 'I'll have a quick shower and change into something cooler. We're going to have fun.'

Marianne wished she could be as certain.

'Trust me.'

The strange thing was she rather thought she did. Putting aside her worries Marianne gave him a big smile and prepared to experience a true Roman evening. Hopefully she wouldn't regret the decision later.

17

'Are you up for walking some more? I'm probably being selfish as I've been cooped up inside all day. If you're tired we can get the train or I can get Francesco to drop us off.' Gabe reappeared, casual in plain linen trousers and a short-sleeved dark blue shirt, but still so handsome it made the breath catch in her throat.

'I'd much prefer to walk. I'm used to being active most of the day and it feels good to want to be again.'

'Good. Let's go.' Gabe wrapped his hand around hers as they left the room and she didn't make any comment, mentally telling herself not to get too used to it.

Today she easily kept up with Gabe's long stride and he kept up a running commentary along the way, surprising her with the depth of his knowledge and obvious love of Italian history.

'How did you meet Carlo?' she asked, recalling the other man's similar passion for the city.

'You mean he seems an unlikely friend?' He flashed her a quick smile. 'After university I spent time in several of our hotels to learn the business. The Vincenzo Bellini was my first and Carlo had just been taken on as part of hotel security. We're the same age and he'd grown up here so I think you could say he showed me the Rome few people see.'

'Including some places your parents wouldn't have approved of?' she teased.

'Maybe.' Gabe grinned. 'I suppose we were young and reckless but Carlo was an imposing figure even then, so we didn't get into much trouble we couldn't get out of.'

'He's very different underneath the scary exterior.' She spoke almost to herself. 'A lot of people are like that aren't they?'

Out of the blue he stopped and fixed

her with his warm eyes, rooting her to the spot. 'You're a good judge of people. You made one slip-up, that's all, so don't beat yourself up the rest of your life.' His hands slid down to rest around her waist. 'I'm not complex.'

She scrutinized his face and saw everything there, openly laid out for anyone to see. 'Good.' It was all she could say for now without showing emotions she wasn't ready to expose. He nodded and they started to walk again.

'That's the Ponte Sisto Bridge.' He pointed to an ancient bridge crossing the Tiber River. 'It was built in the fifteenth century to connect the Trastevere area to the city. It used to be a real working-class place but it's fancied up now and it's the center of Roman nightlife with the best restaurants, bars and shops.'

They walked for ages around the narrow, winding cobbled streets and occasionally stopped to check out some of the interesting small shops. Against her best intentions (and her depleted bank account) she succumbed to the lures of yet another pair of beautiful Italian shoes, this time made of the softest red leather. Out of nowhere they emerged into a large square with yet another beautiful fountain in the center. People swarmed around enjoying the warm summer evening, tourists, locals, and students all mixed together.

'More interesting than Plymouth is it?' Gabe asked mischievously.

'Definitely. This is wonderful.' Spontaneously she hugged him, feeling him resist slightly before closing his arms around her. Resting her head against his chest she allowed herself the indulgence of laying there for a few precious moments.

'So are you,' he murmured against her hair, barely loud enough for her to hear.

Luckily his stomach suddenly growled and Marianne lifted away. 'I think someone is ready for dinner. Are you going to take me to this famous pizza place?'

'Of course, it's across the square and

down a couple of alleys. No one finds it unless they know it's there or they get lost,' he continued smoothly.

'I'm sure that happens a lot.' She'd been baffled by the maze of streets and wouldn't dare to walk around here alone.

He took her arm firmly in his before they set off again. All of a sudden he stopped. 'This is it.'

'Where?' She couldn't see any restaurant.

'There.' Gabe pointed at a small battered sign on the wall where it was just possible to make out the name *Pizzeria Nick and Tony*. 'We walk through the narrow space between the buildings and it's behind.'

'If you say so.' She glanced around but there were only a couple of tourists wandering along the street, staring at their map and probably looking for the same place.

An hour later she sat back in her chair and sighed. 'Goodness. I don't think I'll ever eat pizza in England again. Actually I'm not sure I'll even eat again for a very long time.' Between them they'd demolished a large pizza, topped simply with spinach, prosciutto, hard-boiled egg and peas before being finished off with a light dusting of grated parmesan when it came out of the ancient brick oven. It'd sounded a bizarre combination when Gabe suggested it but she'd fallen in love at the first bite. Washed down with large glasses of ice-cold beer, it was the perfect meal.

'I could suggest gelato but I suspect it'd make you burst, which wouldn't be a pretty sight, even for such a delectable lady.' Gabe grinned. 'How about we walk some more and listen to some of the street entertainers and later on get a drink at my favorite bar?'

She agreed, partly to get away from the desire to never move, to sit here with Gabe forever, drinking in the sight of him across the table and listening to the swirl of rapid Italian going on around them.

'Excuse me a minute. A new text message came in and I'd better check in case it's important.' Gabe's brow furrowed.

'Is everything all right?' Marianne watched as he decided how to answer. 'The truth, Gabe — unless of course it's private and nothing to do with me.'

He passed over his phone. 'Read it yourself and see what you think.'

She's not yours and never will be. Watch your back.

All the energy and joy drained from her and hot tears pressed at her eyes.

'We could report him to the police, but I suspect it wouldn't do much good. There's no real proof of anything,' he stated flatly.

'What am I going to do? I can't live this way.' Her voice shook with frustration.

Gabe's long fingers tapped on the table and then he fixed her with his determined gaze. 'Carlo can deal with this.'

A vision of Robert after a meeting

with Carlo filled Marianne's head. No matter what he'd done she couldn't authorize anything illegal. 'Definitely not.'

'Oh, Marianne, are you suggesting I'd get Carlo to beat him up?' Disappointment filled his eyes.

'Well, I hoped not, but . . . '

He gave a quirky half-smile. 'I think you've read too much about the Sicilian Mafia. We don't all go around cutting off people's fingers, you know, and swearing on our grandfather's blood to get revenge.'

'Then what did you mean? I somehow can't see Carlo sitting down and having a quiet chat with Robert,' she spoke up, determined not to be a pushover.

Gabe's eyes sparkled. 'I've seen that done before, and trust me it works like a charm because people take one look at him and assume the worst.'

'I can't imagine why,' she added dryly.

'Believe it or not Carlo is a computer whiz and a genius at surveillance. He can track down both this message and Robert and we'll end this thing for good. Peacefully.' He held out his hand. 'Agreed?' They shook hands but he didn't let go. 'Would you rather go straight back to the hotel?'

Marianne stuck her chin in the air. 'No. I want to walk and drink and have fun with you.' She refused to allow Robert to continue to affect her life. 'If it's okay with you?'

'Of course. Your wish is my command. I'll forward this to Carlo with an explanation and let him work on it tonight. I'll invite him to join us for an early breakfast to let us know how he got on.' He finished on the phone, snapped it shut and turned to her with a brilliant smile. 'Right, Cinderella, you shall go to the ball. You've asked for fun so that's what you'll get.'

* * *

As the myriads of clocks around the city began to strike midnight a slightly giggly Marianne allowed herself to be steered into the hotel.

'We'll go straight up in the lift,' Gabe insisted. Swiftly he walked them past the manager and wished the man a good night. 'Come on, Cinders.' He unlocked the door and they went inside.

'Well, good evening, dear nephew.'

Marianne's head jerked up to see an attractive woman, dressed in a rich red dressing gown, giving them both a disapproving stare. Gabe instantly dropped her hand and instead greeted his aunt with the traditional kiss on both cheeks.

'My favorite aunt, you're looking more beautiful than ever.'

'And you're as much of a charming rogue as your father,' she declared, but her shining eyes suggested his compliment pleased her.

He smiled and made the introductions. Marianne was instantly engulfed in a wave of subtle perfume and kissed also.

'What a lovely face you have, my dear.' Angelina glanced at Gabe. 'I believe you should call down and order us a tray of coffee.'

'I'd prefer tea if . . . '

'Coffee, black,' Gabe declared in the tone which told her not to argue. 'You'll thank me in the morning.'

'Why do people always say that when they're being priggish?' she retorted.

'Because they're usually right.' He picked up the phone and Marianne found herself being scrutinized by his aunt.

'Let me take a wild guess where my dear nephew took you for the evening. His favorite pizzeria followed by cocktails at the Baccanale?' Marianne nodded and got a knowing smile in return. 'The Baccanale cocktails are famous or infamous depending on how you look at it. It's the best bar in Rome but the fancy display they do making the cocktails muddles your common sense.'

'I only had two mojitos,' Marianne

insisted, sifting through vague recollections of watching the barmen twirling glasses around and mesmerizing the clientele while large TVs blared out the Italy versus Germany football match.

'That's all it takes for me too, but don't worry, you'll be fine.'

A knock on the door announced the room service waiter and soon Gabe passed her a large mug of viciously strong coffee. It burnt her throat and would surely do the same to the lining of her stomach. 'Ugh, that's vile.'

'Drink it, please. If you have a couple glasses of plain water before bed it won't be a problem.' He rubbed his head. 'I should've been more careful with you.'

Marianne didn't want to be pleased at how concerned he was and stifled a smile. She gulped down the rest of the coffee and winced.

'Come on, my dear. I think it's time for bed. Us ladies will take our leave and see you in the morning, Dante.'

Before she could think of protesting,

a wave of tiredness swept over her and she willingly took Angelina's arm and they left Gabe alone.

* ★ ★

The ceiling was strange. Her bedroom at home didn't have ornate decorations of angels and cherubs dancing across it, but for some bizarre reason this one did. Marianne closed her eyes and opened them again. The weird creatures were still there. Slowly it crept back into her brain. Rome. Gabe's hotel.

'Are you awake, Marianna?' The door opened and Angelina stood there. 'Tea?'

'Thank you so much.'

'When you're ready you can join Gabe in the other room for breakfast.'

'Are you not eating with us?'

Angelina shook her head. 'I have to get to work or my slave-driver of a nephew will report me to his father and then I really will be in trouble.' She laughed and Marianne guessed there wasn't a shred of truth in the assertion.

She lay back and enjoyed her tea, thankful for a few moments to collect her thoughts. Next on the agenda was to shower and dress and then she'd face Gabe and whatever the day would bring.

★ ★ ★

Gabe stretched out in one of the oversized chairs and sipped on what she knew would be the first of at least three cups of espresso. 'There you are. Did you sleep well?'

'Yes, thank you. Your aunt was very kind.' A rush of heat flamed her cheeks. 'Thank you for last night.'

He gave her a tender smile. 'You mean for not taking as good a care of you as I should have?'

'It was only two drinks, Gabe. I'm just rather a lightweight where alcohol's concerned, that's all. I'm fine.'

'Good.' He flashed a broad smile. 'Now have some breakfast and we'll tackle the day together.'

231

His words had a nice ring to them and she smiled right back, but immediately a loud knock on the outside door disturbed the moment.

'It must be Carlo. It's a miracle any door survives his strength.'

The brief surge of happiness seeped away; she'd managed to forget about all her problems for a few wonderful hours. Gabe disappeared to answer the door and Marianne prayed they might actually deal with Robert once and for all.

18

Marianne sat back on the sofa and watched Carlo wade through two full plates of cold meats, cheese, hard-boiled eggs and bread, washing it all down with gallons of coffee. She didn't touch a thing herself, deciding the tea plus a large glass of water were all she could face until she knew what he'd discovered about Robert.

'Will that hold you together for a while?' Gabe teased his friend and got a cuff around the head in return.

'You want to hear what I found out or not?' Carlo growled, the gruffness softened by one of his rare smiles, exposing the raft of shiny gold teeth.

'Please,' Marianne said quietly and Gabe slid closer, putting his comforting arm around her shoulder.

'I'd have to say he's not very smart. In fact for someone trying to stay hidden he's dumb. There's a traceable mobile phone and a credit card trail as long as my arm. He traveled to Sicily the day after you arrived and I've easily picked up the hotels he's used and even the flower shop where he ordered the first yellow roses. And yes, he's definitely here now.' Carlo gave a menacing grin. 'Want to know where he's staying?'

'Well, yes, it'd be a help.'

'No need for sarcasm, boss.'

The last word was said in such a joking way Marianne laughed out loud. 'All right, we give in. Amaze us with your genius.'

'I'm glad someone appreciates me.' Carlo mock-glared at Gabe. 'Unlike some ungrateful people I could mention.' He focused on her and turned his back on his supposed friend. 'Your ex-husband is at the Hotel Splendide over on the Via Veneto. It's an expensive place so I assume he's got serious money.'

She frowned. 'Not really. He's got a

reasonably well-paid car sales job, but we've been trying to sell our house since the divorce and in this economy no one's buying. He'll soon be in debt if he keeps this up.'

Carlo gave a seriously evil look. 'Do you want to know where he ate dinner last night?'

'Go on, put us out of our misery,' Gabe interjected.

'The Monte Christo restaurant over in Trastevere.'

Marianne struggled to hold her voice and felt oddly calm. 'So he was probably watching us then too?' Gabe squeezed her hand and she appreciated the warmth of his reassuring touch. 'Let's hope he saw me enjoying myself with you. It'll serve him right,' she stated bluntly.

'What do you want me to do next?' Carlo asked.

'It's up to the lady here, but I'd suggest you track him down and observe from a distance today.' Gabe raised a brow questioningly at her and carried on when she nodded her agreement. 'I've got to work this morning but I should be through by mid-afternoon at the latest.'

'What am I going to do while you're both busy?' Marianne asked.

'I wondered if you'd like to come with me, check out the floor we're renovating and give me your opinion?' Gabe asked.

'In other words keep the little lady out of the way and quiet.' She resented the fact she was in one of the most glorious cities in the world and trapped in a hotel. The two men exchanged exasperated looks.

'Andy charged me with keeping you safe. You can glare as much as you like but with Carlo otherwise engaged you aren't going out by yourself.'

His sudden seriousness threw Marianne off balance. Gabe was a responsible, dutiful man and he wasn't going to put her at risk. Despite herself she admired him a great deal. 'I'm sorry. I didn't mean to be awkward.'

'You could never be that,' he murmured close to her ear. 'I understand your frustration and I'd feel exactly the same if it were me. I'll finish work as fast as possible and we should be able to squeeze in some sightseeing before dinner.'

'You came here to work, not babysit me. I want you to take as long as you need and not worry about me,' she assured him.

'Have you two finished with the sloppy stuff? Some of us have work to do.' Carlo stood and forced his oversized body back into the black jacket he'd taken off to eat. 'I'll send you updates during the day.' He levered up to standing and strode quickly from the room, giving the door another destructive slam on the way out.

Gabe rubbed a hand over his jaw and grimaced. 'I'd better go and shave and smarten up before going to intimidate some more of my staff. I'll be ready in about fifteen minutes if that's okay and then we'll get on.' He glanced humorously at her. 'How's your head?'

'Actually it's not too bad. I might try to eat the pastry Carlo missed, although I'm not sure how it escaped his onslaught. Unless of course you're hungry and would like to have it?'

'Go ahead, you know I'm not a breakfast-eater.' He turned away and headed for the bathroom.

Worry settled back in to Marianne's brain and it killed her appetite in an instant. She wasn't concerned about Carlo, who could plainly take care of himself, but would Robert do something stupid? He'd always been very careful about money, to the point of being almost miserly, so to hear he was throwing it around like he'd won the lottery didn't fit.

'You're over-thinking everything again, aren't you?' Gabe reappeared, freshly shaved and immaculate in yet another beautiful suit. This time it was pale grey and paired today with a deep blue shirt and a patterned silk tie. He could've stepped right off the cover of a magazine and Marianne's heart raced in a very teenage way.

'Not at all.' She eyed him up. 'Going for smooth and menacing today are we? Very sharp and edgy.' Too handsome came to mind as well, but she kept that thought private.

'Good. That's the idea.' He smoothed a hand over his jet-black, close-cut hair and smiled. 'Come on. Let Carlo worry about your erstwhile husband for a while.'

'Sounds good to me.'

The next few hours were a revelation where it came to her view of Gabe. With only a perfunctory knowledge of Italian she still picked up on his level of expertise where the hotel business was concerned. Whether it was dealing with staff problems, bathroom paint colors or financial accounts, he effortlessly coped with it all and her admiration grew. It wasn't his fault he was good-looking; being unattractive didn't necessarily make someone a good person.

'You're doing the heavy thinking thing again, aren't you?'

Gabe's voice nearby startled her and Marianne turned defensive. 'I didn't know I needed permission.'

'Nasty, but I'll ignore you this time.' His arm slipped around her waist as though it belonged there and she didn't pull away. 'We're going to have a working lunch with the different managers here. I need their input on a plan for the next five years where the hotel's concerned. It'll be rather boring for you I'm afraid but the food will be excellent, and I'm guessing you're ready for something by now?'

Marianne realized she was starving. 'Yes, I am and don't worry about me. I'll sit quietly and be the perfect non-interfering companion.' He gave her a non-believing look but didn't comment. She supposed it hadn't been her method so far, having stuck her nose in just about everything from his family to his love life.

Half an hour later she looked around the large round table set in the middle of the dining room and came to the indisputable conclusion that without their hands Italians wouldn't have a clue how to talk. Hands flailed in the air gesticulating and emphasizing every comment they made.

As coffee was being served to everyone a waiter suddenly appeared at her shoulder. '*Scusa*, Signorina. There is a telephone call for you at reception. Are you free to take it?'

'For me?'

The young man nodded agreement and waited for her answer.

'Of course . . . I'll be right out.' She tried to catch Gabe's eye but he was engrossed in explaining something to the catering manager. Discretely pushing back her chair, Marianne left her napkin in the seat and left.

'Let you out of his sight for once did he? It's amusing to know that stupid oversized goon is watching me right now and he has no idea I'm talking to you.'

Robert's steady unemotional voice poured down the phone and she clutched onto the reception desk for support. 'What do you want?' Her voice was a mere whisper.

'You, of course. What did you think?'

'We're divorced. Get it through your head. The papers are signed. Our marriage is over,' Marianne hissed into the phone.

'A mere formality. You're my wife and always will be. You promised in front of about ninety of our closest friends and family. Have you forgotten?'

This would degenerate into another of the around-in-circles arguments they'd had for weeks before she finally left. Robert allowed no logic into his brain where she was concerned.

'I'm hanging up now. Do not call me again because I won't answer.'

'Be at the Baccanale tonight at nine, Marianne, or you'll regret it.'

She forced out a brief laugh. 'Don't

be ridiculous. You're a car salesman not a gangster. Are you planning to kidnap me, or maybe you've paid one of the Mafia to finish me off?'

'Now you're the one being ridiculous.' His voice lowered. 'All I want is to talk to you once more. Make you see sense.'

She checked around to make sure no one was paying attention. If seeing her one more time would finish this then she'd do it, but Gabe mustn't know. This was her problem to sort out. 'All right I'll come, but only for an hour.'

'Fair enough. If I can't persuade you by then I don't deserve you.'

She made no comment.

'I'll see you later, Mrs. Blackwell.'

Marianne didn't respond but merely said goodbye and hung up the phone. For a minute she stood still, allowing herself time to get herself and her expression back to normal. Gabe was far too observant where she was concerned but hopefully he'd be too engrossed in his business meeting to pay her much attention.

'Where did you disappear to?'

Gabe appeared by her side with his arms folded across his broad chest and his dark-eyed gaze fixed hard on her. The wheels turned rapidly in her head as she tried to quickly come up with a reasonable explanation. Someone might mention she had a phone call so she'd use that and stay as close to the truth as possible. 'The waiter came to let me know I had a phone call but it was only Andy checking up on me.' He stared severely for a moment then gave a brief half-smile.

'I see,' he said without conviction.

'Is your meeting finished?' Marianne tried to steer him towards a different topic of conversation.

'Yes, I thought we could change into more casual clothes and do some more sightseeing if you'd like.'

It should work if she went along with him for now and then developed a convenient headache so she could escape on her own. 'Wonderful.' Marianne smiled broadly and swore to throw herself into enjoying the rest of the day until it was time to face Robert. It wouldn't be easy because acting wasn't her forte and Gabe was smart, but she couldn't see any other choice.

★   ★   ★

At least there wasn't any need to fake a headache. After three solid hours of walking around St. Peter's Square, the Basilica and the Sistine Chapel, Marianne was genuinely exhausted. The hot August sun had beaten her and she genuinely wanted nothing more than to lie down in the nice cool hotel room.

'Would I be right in guessing you've had enough of playing tourist for today?' Gabe smiled.

'I'm afraid so. I hate to miss it all, but . . . '

He patted her hand. 'You'll be back. It's impossible to do it all in a few days. Let's head back to the hotel. We can rest then go out for dinner later.'

She needed to make her move now before he made any more plans. 'I'll have to see. I might not feel up to going out.'

Gabe checked his messages while they spoke and his expression turned serious in the middle of reading one.

'Is everything okay?'

'Of course. Is there any reason it wouldn't be?' He asked rather intently and she blushed, afraid he was mind-reading again.

'Not at all, but you seemed concerned.'

'An old friend heard I was in the city and wondered if I could join him for dinner. I'll give our regrets and meet him another time I'm here.'

Marianne gave silent thanks. She hadn't expected to be this lucky. 'Please don't do that. I'll be fine. I can order room service and spend a quiet evening reading. To be honest I'd prefer it. You go out and enjoy yourself.'

'Are you sure?' he asked very quietly

and it took all her courage to meet his steady calm eyes and lie.

'Absolutely.'

Gabe sent a message back then closed his phone. 'That's settled then. I'll head out about eight.'

'I'm sure I'll be asleep by then anyway. I'll leave a message for your aunt so she doesn't worry where I am if she comes in.' She felt terrible. Gabe didn't deserve her disloyalty but maybe after tonight she'd be free to think about the future. The idea was beyond liberating, but she still had to face Robert first. 'Let's go.'

19

Everything about the area looked different tonight. She'd been sensible and taken one of the official white taxis from the hotel instead of trying to walk as she'd done with Gabe. Marianne purposely asked to be dropped off in the Piazza Santa Maria in case her destination got reported back later on. She'd have to say she felt better and decided to return to the same place for dinner. It was the best explanation she could come up with and hoped it wouldn't be necessary. She should easily be back in the hotel and tucked up in bed long before Gabe returned.

She stared all around and struggled to remember which of the narrow streets they'd walked down to find the bar. The crowds were heavier tonight and she was jostled continually. It made her nervous and she clung on to her handbag while trying not to look like a dumb lost tourist.

All of a sudden Marianne thought she spotted a familiar alley and headed purposefully across the square. After making a couple of turns, the white awning Gabe pointed out last night appeared on her right. Cautiously she stepped inside, overwhelmed by the noise and waves of heat emanating from the crowd of people. She tried to appear unconcerned and checked out the room looking for Robert.

Over in the far corner the light reflected off a man's pale gold hair and she let out the breath she'd unconsciously been holding. She should've guessed Robert would already be here and waiting. Marianne wove her way through the tightly crammed-together tables and tried not to bump anyone as she went.

Robert glanced straight at her and immediately jumped up. 'Marianne, my dear, you're looking particularly beautiful tonight.' He bent down and kissed her cheek, his unexpected touch making her flinch. Marianne hoped he wouldn't notice but the instant change from warm to ice-cold in his sky-blue eyes told her he had. She could never hide anything from him. 'Would you care for a cocktail?'

'Just an orange juice please.' Marianne didn't really want anything but it'd give her something to do with her hands. He headed for the bar and she slid into the empty chair next to his.

'So, my dear, where's your boyfriend tonight?' He set a tall glass of ruby-red blood orange juice down in front of her and sat down, pulling the chair closer than necessary.

'Not that it's any of your business, but I don't have a boyfriend.'

'Don't play me for a fool,' he sneered. 'I assume I was supposed to think you're going out with that muscle-bound thug, but I'm not stupid. He's not at all your type.'

She took a sip of her juice and didn't attempt to defend Carlo.

'Last evening I saw you with Alessandro. Rather an obvious sort of man I'd say.'

Marianne rested her hands in her lap. 'He's an old friend of Andy's. I came here for a break before school starts, that's all.'

He carried on as though she hadn't spoken. 'I suppose he's taking pity on the poor broken-hearted divorcee. How touching.'

'This is pointless. Why did you ask me to come here? We have nothing more to say to each other.' She picked up her handbag but Robert seized her wrist. 'Ow.'

'Do not move. I haven't told you we're through yet.'

She glanced anxiously around them but no one appeared to be paying them any attention.

'Don't get any smart ideas.' Robert eased the pressure on her wrist and leaned in closer. 'I have a taxi waiting. We'll go to your hotel and collect your belongings. You will check out and leave a message for Signor Alessandro to say you've been urgently called back home.'

About to ask if he was crazy, Marianne stared into his cold empty eyes and bit back her words.

'That's better. Maybe you're learning to behave like a proper wife at last.'

Not angering him any further was her best move until she could come up with a way to escape.

'Now, we will get up and leave and I don't expect you to indicate we're anything less than a loving couple. Do I make myself clear?'

She nodded and forced herself not to pull away when he took hold of her hand. Once she'd enjoyed his touch, until she'd come to associate it with mockery and unkindness. As they stepped outside and the cooler air hit her face she panicked, afraid this might be her last chance.

'Planning something, are you?' Robert snatched her handbag and rifled through it. 'Are you looking for this?' He waved around her mobile phone before turning it off and slipping it into his pocket.

'Not at all. I'm just being careful with all these pickpockets around.'

'Here's the car.' He steered her towards a white taxi, opened the door and pushed her into the back seat.

'I don't think the lady wants to go.' Carlo's deep voice resonated close by and in a second Robert fell to the ground and yelled as the larger man held him in place.

'Are you all right, *tesoro*, my darling?' Gabe appeared in front of her, his face etched with worry, and helped her out of the car. The taxi driver ranted at them and waved his arms around, clearly asking for money. She guessed Gabe's reply told him he was lucky they weren't calling the police and he'd better drive away while he still could.

'How did you know . . . ?' Her words trailed away as hot, fat tears rolled down her cheeks.

'Long story, but the GPS Carlo put on your phone works whether it's turned on or not. We'll discuss the rest later.'

Marianne swallowed hard, not looking forward to that conversation.

'My limousine is around the corner. Let's get this useless creature back to the hotel and decide what to do with him.' Gabe gestured at Robert and Carlo hauled him upright with one hand then practically dragged him along the pavement.

In the back of the car Marianne rested her head on Gabe's shoulder, grateful for his solid warmth, but they didn't talk. At the hotel nobody commented as they walked up to the reception desk and Gabe issued a quick request for coffee to be sent up to his suite. Another couple were all set to step in the lift but took one look at the four of them and declared they'd changed their minds and preferred to walk.

As they entered the room Carlo tossed Robert down on the sofa and went over to stand over by the door.

'Mister Blackwell, I'm not wasting my time asking what you were going to do with Marianne tonight. You are divorced and she has made it perfectly clear she wants nothing more to do with you.' Robert tried to interrupt but Gabe snapped his fingers. 'Be quiet until I ask you to speak. I will tell you your choices. You can get the next plane to London, resign your job in Plymouth and move a significant distance away. After that you will never contact Marianne again in any way. If you don't agree I will call the police now and let them deal with you. I believe stalking and attempted kidnapping should put you in prison long enough to bring you to your senses. We've kept records of everything you've done to bother her while she's been in Italy. Also if you choose the first option and don't follow through the police will be told everything.'

All the fight went out of Robert and he slumped forward, his head dropping down into his hands. After a minute he glanced back up and stared at her. 'Is this really what you want, my darling?' His voice was shaky and unsure.

Marianne took a deep breath before answering. 'Yes, Robert. I'm sorry it's come to this.'

His attention switched back to Gabe. 'I accept your first offer.'

'I've booked you a seat on the early flight out in the morning. Carlo will take you to a hotel near the airport and make sure you don't miss the plane.'

'You can trust me. I don't need a bodyguard,' Robert insisted.

In an obvious gesture of possession Gabe slid his arm around her shoulders. 'Marianne needs to be sure. You've put her through enough.'

Robert gave a weak smile and conceded. He tried to stand and stumbled a little before Gabe grasped his elbow to steady him. 'Goodbye, my love.'

She couldn't answer but she followed him with her eyes as he limped towards the door and left with Carlo.

'I do believe this calls for some grappa. Coffee isn't going to do the trick.' Without waiting for an answer Gabe strode over to the bar and poured them both a large measure of the fiery liquid. He downed his in one swallow and she followed his example, determined not to choke.

'You want an explanation for tonight.' She made it a statement not a question.

'It'd be nice.' Gabe said nothing else, lay back on the sofa and stretched out his long legs.

'Maybe I should apologize, but I believed it was my problem to solve and felt I'd dragged you into enough of my troubles already.'

'Did I ever complain?' he asked in a steady voice, totally unlike his normal, more expressive manner.

'No.'

'I understand you've had enough of a man telling you what to do.'

'Yes, but . . . ' This wasn't going how she'd expected. 'You're not that way.'

'Good.'

Marianne played with one of the wood coasters, spinning it idly and wasting time while she decided where to go next with the awkward conversation. 'When did you know I was planning something?'

'When the waiter told me your call came from here in Rome although you said it was from England.'

'You checked up on me?' A rush of anger flared through her body.

'I was worried. You'd have been happy if Andy rang, but you weren't. I could see the strain here — ' His finger touched the corner of her eye. ' — and here.' It moved to her lips.

'Am I really so obvious?'

For the first time during the evening his face lit up with the ghost of a smile. 'Yes.'

'And after you knew?'

'Carlo was still tracking Robert's phone and intercepted the message.' He held up his hand as she started to protest. 'Be mad at me if you like, but I was sure he hadn't given up and was concerned. I don't mind admitting I wasn't happy, Marianna.'

By the tautness in his voice she guessed it went far deeper and felt so guilty. 'You have every right not to be.'

'Maybe, maybe not. I made it easy for you and invented a reason to go out.'

'There was no old friend?'

He shook his head. 'No, and I arranged with the hotel for a reliable taxi if you ordered one. Carlo and I made our plans.' Touching her arm, his voice sunk to a whisper. 'I was in the bar and watched you go to him. When he touched you . . . I still don't know how I stopped myself pulling him away.'

'You've got more self-control than you give yourself credit for.'

'It nearly failed me tonight,' he admitted.

'I can't believe I didn't see you.'

'You weren't looking for me, plus I don't stand out in a crowd of Italians.'

She needed to get this over with for both their sakes. 'I'm ready with my apology now. It was stupid, thoughtless and disrespectful of me.'

Gabe gave a tentative half-smile. 'Are you ready to step away from the past or am I rushing you again?'

Answering him was difficult, she wanted so much to agree. 'Tonight was hard for me, Gabe. Can you be patient a little longer?'

'As long as you want. I told you so before and I meant it. We'll go back to Sicily tomorrow. I've some things to talk about with my father, then at the weekend we'll take our delayed trip to Taormina if my aunt and uncle are agreeable. Does it sound like a plan to you?'

Marianne nodded, unable to speak. Could she really trust and love again? She had a feeling the weekend would prove it one way or the other.

20

'Your father is driving me mad. For goodness sake go and talk about the business to him and take his mind off of his leg.'

Sofia grabbed Gabe firmly by the elbow and steered him into the house. With a quick glance back over his shoulder he gave Marianne an apologetic smile, but she didn't mind. After the last few days being back here was a relief, although she hoped to return to Rome in the future and see more of the fascinating city. She said a quick hello to Caterina and headed up the spiral staircase to her bedroom.

For a few blissful minutes she lay on the bed and did absolutely nothing. It crossed her mind to call Andy, but he could wait until tomorrow because he'd want too many details and she wasn't in the mood. Her mind fixed on Gabe and for the first time she allowed the idea of a future with him into her head. She certainly found it hard to imagine one without him, which had to be a sign.

'Signorina Westlake, you have a visitor.' Caterina's voice interrupted her musings and she got up to open the door.

'Who wants me?'

'Signorina Rossini.'

'For me? Are you sure?' It seemed very unlikely but Caterina must know what she was talking about.

'Yes. She particularly asked to see you alone and not with Signor Dante.'

'Oh, well all right. Tell her I'll be down in a few minutes.' At the very least she needed to pull a comb through her hair and put on some lipstick before facing the gorgeous model. 'Would you mind bringing us some tea on the terrace? It might help.' Caterina nodded and went back downstairs.

★ ★ ★

'Hello, Alexandra. This is a pleasant surprise.' Marianne was amazed she didn't get struck down by lightning on the spot for such a blatant lie.

'I am sorry to bother you when you have just returned, but I could not wait any longer.'

'Would you care for some tea?' If nothing else it'd give them something to do. She took the lack of an answer as agreement and poured out two cups before pushing one across the table to her erstwhile guest.

Alexandra took one sip then set down the cup. 'I must say what I came here to tell you or I will lose the nerve as you English say.' She gripped the table and went quite pale under her beautiful dark gold skin. 'It is my fault Signor Blackwell found you in Rome.'

'Your fault? But you don't even know Robert.'

'I am afraid I do. Let me speak, please.' Alexandra rushed on. 'The first night I met you I left in a hurry and

263

drove back down to Catania. Apparently he'd been watching this house and followed me. I was very angry and stopped to get a drink at an outdoor café. He approached me and was very charming.' A rush of heat colored her cheeks.

'He can be,' Marianne said dryly.

'We talked and he kept buying me drinks. The next thing I am telling him all about Dante and how badly he'd treated me. He asked me out for dinner the next night and that's when he admitted knowing you.'

'I'm sure he put me in a bad light where our marriage was concerned.'

Alexandra nodded. 'Of course. I was willing to believe everything he said. Robert encouraged me to see myself as a victim. I came here to visit Dante's father and he said you'd gone to Rome together that morning. It made me angry and when I rang Robert to complain he was very sympathetic and spun a good story about how he wanted you back and needed the chance to speak to you.' Her gaze dropped away to the table and she slowly crumbled a biscotti between her manicured fingers. 'I convinced myself I was doing you a favor by telling him where you were staying.'

'You might care to know he's been harassing me ever since I've been here.' It was a struggle to keep her voice steady. 'In Rome he attempted to make me leave with him, but luckily Gabe and his friend stopped him.'

Alexandra's hand flew up to cover her mouth. 'Oh, no, I would never have . . . ' Tears glistened in her eyes.

'It's all right. He'll leave me alone now and everything is good, I promise.'

The Italian woman's chin tilted up defiantly. 'What about you and Dante?'

Marianne tried to give her an honest answer. 'I'm not sure yet. I didn't come here intending to spoil anything between you.'

'If it was meant to be you wouldn't have been successful. I've been fooling myself for a long time and Dante let me. That was not fair of him.'

'No, it wasn't, and I owe you a huge apology.' Gabe stood in the doorway, his face strained and tired. 'You didn't deserve to be treated so badly.'

'How long have you been there?' Marianne swung around and stared at him.

'Long enough.'

'Would you prefer to speak privately with Alexandra?'

'There's no need for my sake, Marianne,' Alexandra insisted. 'There is nothing left between us which cannot be said in front of other people. Our families know how things are, I am ready to move on and I'm sure Dante is too. I'm off to Paris in the morning for a couple of weeks' work, which is why I came today.'

'I really am sorry. I never intended to hurt you,' Gabe said sadly.

'I know, but it still doesn't excuse my behavior with Signor Blackwell which was why I had to straighten things out.' She stood up and prepared to leave and Marianne joined her by the door.

'Thank you. I appreciate your honesty and wish you nothing but the best.'

'Me too.' Gabe stepped forward and kissed his former girlfriend on both cheeks. 'Is it too clichéd to say I hope we can still be friends?'

'No, but it is too soon.' Her eyes rested tenderly on him and when she spoke her voice was wistful. 'I'm sure one day I can visit and we will remember the past happily, but not yet. Goodbye.' She stepped away and headed back into the house before either of them could prolong things.

'I'm sorry, Marianna. Sorry for treating her so thoughtlessly, and sorry it led to you going through even more distress. I do not deserve for you to forgive me but I'm going to ask you to anyway.'

His pleading gaze tugged at her heart. Slowly she took hold of his hands and stared into his dark emotion-filled eyes. 'That is behind us now in the same way Robert is behind us. Our next challenge is finding the best way to go on.'

'Together I hope?'

'I hope so too.' She smiled. 'How about we start by spending the weekend in Taormina? I don't know about you but I could do with working off some physical energy and just plain relaxing.'

'Sounds good to me. I'll get things organized. I promised my father I'd take him to the doctor for his X-ray tomorrow morning but we could leave straight after.'

'What about work?'

He frowned. 'I'll inform him I'm taking a few days off. If he objects it's unfortunate. I'll talk to him more about work when we return.'

She almost asked what exactly the conversation would be about but held her tongue. Things were slowly sorting out. She needed to be patient too.

* * *

The warm breeze caught Marianne's hair as she glanced over at Gabe, casual in shorts and a black t-shirt, his

268

competent hands steering them down the narrow, winding roads just a little too fast. Conversation was impossible over the roar of the engine so she lay back and gave herself up to the moment. As they paralleled the stunning coastline she paid more attention and took in every changing view of the sapphire blue Mediterranean, storing it up in her mind for when she was back in cold, grey Plymouth. Turning off the main road they slowed down, heading along a deserted narrow road which unexpectedly dead-ended in front of a huge white villa perched on a cliff overlooking the ocean.

'Here we are.' He blew the car horn and the gates slowly swung open, obviously opened from inside.

'I thought you described it as a small house they keep for a weekend getaway.'

'Did I?' Gabe grinned. 'By some standards it is.'

'Not mine,' she said ruefully while secretly loving the place already.

'Do you want to go back home?' he teased, his face full of mischief.

'Not likely,' Marianne retorted.

He laughed and drove on in around the winding driveway and up to the front door.

The next hour blurred as they were swept inside by Nico's brother, Luciano. Marianne decided she was far too vulnerable to the Alessandro men's charm as she fell under the spell of yet another one. His wife was out shopping with a girlfriend but would return in time for them all to dine together. Luciano took them on a guided tour of the beautiful house, with its pure white décor, perfectly accented by bright colored artwork and terracotta tiled floors.

'I show you to your rooms and you can rest before dinner. We usually eat around eight, if that suits you both?' Luciano asked and proceeded to show them the way.

★ ★ ★

Later they sat alone on the terrace after a delicious meal and watched the sun set, a flaming ball sinking down over the glittering sea. Luciano and Anna had retired to bed and told them to stay up as long as they liked. Gabe opened another bottle of Prosecco and poured them both a glass.

'Do you fancy doing some snorkeling in the morning and then after lunch hit the beach to have a go on the jet-skis?' Gabe asked.

'It sounds amazing. I suppose you've done both before?'

'A fair amount. I love throwing myself into anything physically challenging. Rock climbing, parachuting, scuba diving, wakeboarding, water-skiing — anything really.' His voice resonated with enthusiasm for the day ahead and Marianne saw his true passion for the first time.

'Would you mind if I had an early night? It's been a long few days and I suspect I might actually sleep well here.'

'Of course,' Gabe murmured and

leaned closer to slide his hand down her cheek. 'I need you to realize how deeply you make me feel.' He eased his fingers through the silky strands of her hair and pulled them both up to standing.

'Gabe, I . . . '

'Don't say it tonight, my love. Go and get some sleep.' Very tenderly he pushed her away. 'If you want to wear an attractive bikini tomorrow I won't object.'

'You're hopeless, Dante Gabriele Alessandro.'

'Precisely. I'm a prime candidate for reformation.' His exaggerated wink made her giggle.

'And you think I'd take on the job?'

'I suspect you're well qualified. The question is whether you're brave enough?'

'I'll let you know when I decide.' An undercurrent of things unsaid ran through their flirtatious exchange. 'Good night.'

Gabe nodded but stayed silent as his eyes followed her out of sight. Marianne didn't think she'd sleep much tonight. There was too much on her mind and tomorrow to wonder about.

21

Marianne swam lazily through the warm, crystal-clear water and relished the sights around her: vivid tropical fish, bright orange coral and myriads of shrimps. She'd snorkeled before, but nowhere like this amazing paradise. As she turned she caught Gabe's eye and they shared another of those moments it was getting harder to ignore. He flashed an OK sign and led them further into the Blue Grotto, pointing out rainbow fish and some eels on the way. Luciano's private boat waited for them outside so there was no having to wait for other tourists or rush to return to shore because everyone else was ready.

Reluctantly they left, swam back to the boat and climbed in. Marianne stretched out in the sun to dry off, drinking down the cold bottle of water

Gabe passed from the cooler in a couple of long swallows.

'Ready for lunch?'

She nodded, unable to believe she was hungry already.

'Luigi's going to pull in to Naxos and we'll eat at one of the restaurants on the lido. I could ask if you enjoyed yourself but it was obvious, *tesoro*, darling.'

His broad genuine smile touched her heart and impulsively she reached up and kissed him lightly on the cheek.

'I'm glad you liked it but we'd better not frighten Luigi.' He let his hands drop away and stepped backwards. His gruff whisper brought her back to common sense.

'I'm sorry, Gabe. I didn't mean to . . . '

'*Amore mio*, it tells me you care very deeply and that gives me hope.'

She touched her finger to his lips. 'Thank you.' Marianne gave him a bright smile. 'Now what about lunch? I'm starving.' He nodded and asked for the boat to go in to shore. As they pulled up onto the beach he leapt out and grasped her hand to steady her as she stepped onto the hot golden sand.

'I promise you shall have the best calamari in the world.'

Of course he was right and two hours later they finished the most wonderful lunch of Marianne's life.

'You didn't take my advice.' Gabe trailed a finger down the strap of her plain, emerald-green one-piece swim-suit.

'I wasn't sure a bikini would stand up to your adventurous plans.'

Gabe lay back in the chair and studied her for a minute before speaking. 'I think we'd better get back out on the water, don't you? Come on.' He held out his hand and they stood up to walk away from the crowded lido. 'Luciano's jet-skis are down this way.' He pointed towards a small dock at the far end of the beach.

'He's got his own?'

'Yes, several. I'd buy one myself but I don't get down here enough to make it worthwhile.' She caught a hint of frustration in his voice but didn't comment. 'There we go. Isn't she a beauty?'

A glossy blue and white jet-ski sat ready for them, watched over by a young Sicilian holding lifejackets. Marianne was relieved to see it was a two-seater so she wouldn't have to drive herself. After a brief conversation Gabe dispatched the other man and handed her one of the lifejackets.

'Don't worry, I'll start off slow. We have to anyway until we get out from the shore. Of course after that I'll liven things up a bit.' He flashed her a wicked grin.

'Not too much. You car scares me enough,' she insisted, but he only laughed.

'I'll get you addicted to speed yet.' Gabe eased the jet-ski into the water and straddled the seat. 'Hop on and hold on.'

Marianne jumped on the back and slid her arms around his waist and he started up the engine, steering them carefully out into the sheltered bay. He'd warned her they'd do some gentle turns to get her used to shifting her weight with the jet-ski before really taking off.

Briefly he glanced behind and gave her a broad smile before turning up the throttle and increasing their speed. The jet-ski's nose rose out of the water and they approached a wave head-on, spraying her face and making her lift slightly from the seat. Her heart raced and a thrill surged through her as they sliced through the waves at high speed. She realized they were slowing down to head back in to shore and far too soon Gabe brought them carefully into the dock and cut the engine.

'You can let go now,' he teased, gesturing towards her hands still clutched tightly around him.

'Sorry.'

'I'm not, but unfortunately we can't sit here all day while poor Mario waits to put this superb toy away.'

She hadn't noticed the boy waiting for them. Marianne apologized again but he brushed it off.

'What did you think of that?'

'I loved it. I could happily do that every day — it's amazing,' she enthused. 'In fact this whole day's been wonderful.'

'It's not finished yet,' Gabe answered. 'I thought we might rest back at the lido a while, have a cold drink and take in some sun. Luigi could take us for a trip along the coast again later and pull in somewhere for dinner.'

'What about your aunt and uncle? Won't they be expecting us to join them?'

He shook his head. 'They're dining out with friends tonight and said they'd see us later.'

'In that case I'd love to.'

'Would you prefer to go back to the villa and change first? Not that your swimsuit isn't charming of course.'

Marianne smacked his arm. 'You're impossible. Changing would be good.'

278

Back at the lido they settled on a couple of sun loungers and ordered tall glasses of fruity sangria. Marianne couldn't help but think this was as close to perfect as life could be. The hot sun on her skin, the glistening Mediterranean, Gabe stretched out next to her and the sound of children's laughter playing nearby. Plymouth and her classes seemed a very long way off.

'Oh.' She jumped up as a large ball hit her square in the center of the stomach.

'*Scusa.*' A red-faced little girl in a yellow frilly swimsuit and matching flip-flops stood there with tears spilling from her dark soulful eyes.

'It's all right.' Marianne glanced over at Gabe who instantly translated for her. 'Please tell her not to worry.' The girl chattered on, still upset.

'She says she is playing catch with her brother but always misses the ball and he teases her. Her friends do too and she hates playing games in school because they all laugh at her.'

'Oh, Gabe, that's sad.' Marianne gazed around. 'Are her family here? I'd love to help her learn if they'd allow it.'

Suddenly an elegant dark-haired woman in a smart red bathing suit walked over and began talking to Gabe. They had quite a conversation but Marianne couldn't understand more than the occasional word. He turned back to her.

'I told Signora Grazio what you said and she is very appreciative. They have to leave in an hour, but you're welcome to play with little Giada until then. She says they've tried to show her what to do but she's clumsy. Are you sure you want to do this?'

'Yes, I'd love to. It's not hard, Gabe, and it'll give her confidence. You might have to help me if I need to verbally explain anything. Can you go over to the shop and find a smaller ball that's soft? I'm guessing she's been hit by this one more than once, which can be scary.'

He willingly agreed and soon Giada's

mother went back to her family nearby, where they could keep an eye on her but not close enough to put her off.

Marianne guessed the girl was maybe five, the same age as her reception class pupils. She sat down on the sand with her legs spread and indicated for Giada to sit the same way. Very slowly she rolled the new pink ball into the girl's open hands and got her to roll it back. They did this for a while until Marianne moved up on her knees and got the child to copy her again. She tossed the ball gently into Giada's hands and her brilliant smile when she caught it the first time tugged at Marianne's heart. Gradually she shuffled back and put more distance between them. Marianne stood and the girl immediately did the same. She encouraged Giada to spread her legs further apart for better balance and then moved to stand closer again to start off. The girl dropped the first ball and Marianne held her breath hoping they wouldn't have a fit of tears.

'It's okay. Everyone drops them at first. We'll try again as many times as you want to.' The next one Giada caught and the next, so it didn't bother her as much when another dropped. Every few minutes Marianne moved further away without making a big deal of it. The girl's smile grew broader with each success and she even managed to laugh off the few failures.

Signora Grazio reappeared and started clapping her hands. Giada ran into her arms for a big hug and the mother instantly launched into a torrent of rattled Italian.

'She says you are wonderful. She wishes you lived here so you could teach her some more,' Gabe translated.

'Are you sure you didn't make up the last bit?'

'No, but I've had a brilliant idea. We'll talk back at the house.' His voice hummed with barely suppressed excitement.

'Thank her from me and say Giada's a wonderful little girl.'

He immediately did as she asked and the child threw her arms around Marianne, giving her a warm hug before her mother told her they needed to leave.

Gabe hastily gathered up their belongings and they walked towards the car at his usual fast speed. 'Do you want to shower and change before we talk?'

Somehow she thought it might be a good idea. If nothing else it'd give him time to calm down before regaling her with some ridiculous idea. 'Yes, please. Fairly casual for tonight I assume?'

'Yes, no high heels for climbing in and out of the boat, although if you like to wear some it'll give me an excuse to help you.'

'You're hopeless.'

He pretended to look contrite but it was so patently fake she gave up and settled into the car ready for the drive back to the villa.

* * *

'You look so pretty. That color really suits you.' Gabe's dark eyes gleamed with obvious appreciation as she came back into the living room. She'd wondered if the sunshine-yellow dress with its nipped in waist and flared skirt was too much but his obvious approval confirmed it'd been a good choice.

'Thank you.'

'I've got wine and a few snacks ready out on the terrace. I did ask my uncle to join us but he's busy in his study.' He gestured towards the open French doors and led her out to a tiled patio covering the full width of the house.

They sat at the small white table, sheltered by a charming pink and white striped umbrella. Right in front of them was a hedge of fragrant bright pink tropical flowers and beyond that the sheer rugged cliffs dropped down towards the sparkling sea.

For a few minutes they sipped on their favorite Prosecco and nibbled salty olives and crispy Parmesan crackers.

'I've been thinking.' Gabe fixed his attention on her.

'Dangerous,' she joked.

'Now, now, be nice. I hardly know where to start but I'll try with what came to me this afternoon. You're a brilliant teacher and great with children. I also saw how much you enjoyed the water sports we did earlier. Am I right on both scores?'

'Well, yes, it's been one of my best days ever.'

'Good. Same for me.' He took hold of her right hand, idly playing with her fingers and destroying her concentration. 'Hypothetically speaking, do you think you would like teaching children water sports and other activities while they were on holiday?'

'Yes, but . . . '

'No buts for a minute. It'd be fun to build a small resort hotel for families. Very personal and friendly with plenty of things to do for everyone. It can be hard work holidaying with children, but ours wouldn't be. The catering would vary from gourmet for the parents to familiar for the children. I'm sure you'd be ideal to run the activities with me. We'd get a good manager to help so we'd have plenty of free time as well.'

Ignoring a myriad of other questions, she asked the obvious one. 'What about the fact I don't speak Italian?'

He waved his hand dismissively. 'You'd soon learn and your English would be a plus to attract English families. Do you speak any other languages?'

'Enough French and German for most children.'

Gabe beamed. 'See, perfect.'

She hesitated over what to say next, but there was no choice in her mind. 'What exactly are you asking me? To come here and run a resort with you as business partners, or something more personal?'

His eyes darkened. 'Are you ready for me to ask for more?'

Marianne smiled and nodded. 'Yes, much more.'

'I want to date you properly, openly, and for the sake of my sanity not for too long.' He suddenly looked shy and unsure of himself. 'If you still feel the same afterwards . . . '

'Gabe. I don't know how you feel about independent, strong women, but I'm going to take a chance. I appreciate you trying to take it slowly, but I love you and I don't want to do slow.' Marianne took hold of his hands and stared into his slightly bemused eyes. 'Dante Gabriele Alessandro, will you marry me?'

A stunned silence fell between them and for a second she panicked. Suddenly he seized hold of her and proceeded to kiss her very thoroughly until she had no breath left. Gasping slightly, she laughed out loud. 'Was that a yes?'

'Yes, yes, yes, you crazy English-woman. If you're going to keep on surprising me we're going to have the most fun, unpredictable marriage ever.'

'What about . . . '

'Details later, *amore mio*. Right now we're going to celebrate.'

Marianne was happy to let him take charge. Nothing was going to spoil the perfect day, even if tomorrow might be another thing.

22

'You know Gabe extremely well — he was your best friend for heaven's sake — so why are you being this way?' Marianne pestered Andy, ready to tear her hair out in frustration.

'What's that to do with marrying him?' he retorted. 'He's a great guy, but let's just say he enjoys women a lot.'

She sighed. 'I'm sure you played the field too. Don't lie and tell me your darling wife was your first and only girlfriend.'

'Come off it, Squib, you know Gabe's a charmer through and through.'

'You haven't seen him in about ten years. He's matured the same as you have. Why did you trust him enough to ask for help and send me here if that's how you feel about him?'

Andy didn't speak for several long seconds.

'You're right and I'm sorry. I knew I could rely on him even though we hadn't been in touch. I suppose I'm wary for your sake because of Robert. Maybe I shouldn't say this but you swore you loved him too and were certain he was Mr. Right. Do you really blame me for urging you to be cautious?' Andy asked.

Hearing the concerned love in his voice touched her. 'No, and I appreciate it, but this is different. Trust me, please. I'm coming back next week to sort out things at school.'

'Are you sure about moving to Sicily? This hotel thing sounds a crazy idea. Everything's happened so fast and Mum and Dad are worried you know.'

'It's what we both want. Gabe will soon reassure you all when you see him.'

'He's coming with you?'

'Of course. I've got to show him off as well as the ring, haven't I?' She laughed, checking out her left hand and happily turning the stunning sapphire and diamond band to catch the light better.

'Okay, I give in.'

Andy sounded resigned, not exactly the emotion she'd hoped for but it'd have to do for now. So far her family was underwhelmed by her engagement and she only hoped they'd get a better reaction from Gabe's family.

★ ★ ★

'Engaged? Rather quick isn't it, son?' Nico Alessandro frowned as Gabe informed them of their exciting news. 'You haven't known each other long as adults and marriage is a serious commitment. I don't mean to offend you, Marianne, but you have been married once already which somewhat concerns me for Dante's sake.'

Gabe's face suddenly turned very stern and unsmiling. 'I will not have my fiancée insulted this way. She couldn't have known what Robert was like and was right to get out of the situation.' He squeezed her hand reassuringly before turning back to his father. 'You told me once you were already engaged when you met Mamma. How long was it before you broke things off and proposed, two weeks or three?'

She got an unseemly pleasure from seeing his parents blush.

'I don't see that's relevant,' Nico insisted.

'Why not? We're completely certain of our love for each other so why should we have to wait some officially sanctioned suitable time, when you didn't? Did it turn out so terribly for you?'

Sofia touched her husband's arm. 'He's right, Nico. You stormed all over my father when he said you weren't good enough for me and wouldn't give his permission. Have you forgotten?'

His eyes softened as he met her loving glance. 'No, my love, I haven't. I didn't mean to be the heavy-handed father.' Nico stared hard at his only child. 'You're all we have. I probably overreacted.' Seeing his son's unmoving expression he shrugged. 'Okay I did overreact. No question about it.'

Sofia walked across and kissed Gabe on both cheeks before doing the same to Marianne. 'I wish you every happiness in the world. I've no regrets about our fast decision and after thirty-five years I'd marry your father again tomorrow.' She stared at Nico and Marianne watched him take the hint.

'Absolutely. She drives me to distraction but I couldn't imagine being without her. She makes my life worth living.' He held open his arms and Gabe drew him into a long, hard hug. 'Now we're going to open the special bottle of champagne I've been saving and you'll tell us all your plans.'

A short while later Marianne didn't blame Nico for looking shaken. He might've suspected Gabe didn't want to take over the hotel empire but she supposed he'd hoped to be wrong. Hearing it spelled out must be hard but he gave the appearance of taking it well, which was the most they could hope for today.

'I'm sure you'll make a big success of this, both of you.' He lifted his glass to them.

Gabe held her hand. 'We think so too. We want a better balance in our lives. To work hard, but play hard too and most importantly to build a family together.' He glanced at her for back-up.

'You put it perfectly.'

★　★　★

Much later they finally sat alone on the terrace where it'd all begun. An empty bottle of Prosecco stood on the table between them and Marianne snuggled into Gabe's warm shoulder. As the inky darkness settled around them the sky suddenly lit up with exploding bursts of gold and red fireworks.

'What are they in honor of tonight?' Marianne asked.

'The forthcoming marriage of Dante Gabriele Alessandro and Marianne

Elizabeth Westlake.' Gabe smiled broadly and kissed the back of her neck.

'You are silly.'

'I'm perfectly serious. Caterina told me earlier and she's never wrong.' His dark eyes sparkled with mischief.

'For once I won't argue.'

'That'll make a change.' He silenced her instant attempt to protest with another kiss, adding to the fireworks display in Marianne's heart. 'Oh, turn around, *amore mio*.' He pointed up towards the mountain behind them.

Fierce columns of red flew up into the night sky and thin paths of hot lava rolled down the dark slopes. 'See, my other woman is pleased. She's celebrating with us. Now we have her approval, everything is good.'

And it was.

THE END

ONE LAKELAND SUMMER

Teresa Ashby

Camping on a farm in the Lake District following a successful business trip, young American Mike Carter Junior sees the farmer's daughter, Amy Palmer, for the first time and falls instantly head-over-heels in love. But Mike is due back in the States, where his fiancée Kari Reynolds is finalising the arrangements for their wedding. Then Kari travels to the Lakes to win her fiancé back. Meanwhile, Mike's arrival has set off a chain of events that could well end in tragedy . . .

WITH LOVE FROM AUNT RUBY

Catriona McCuaig

When her engagement to Tom Carson is broken off, Alyssa Grant exchanges city life for an extended stay in the small Canadian town where her elderly Aunt Ruby is recovering from an injury. Ruby, a retired schoolteacher who is determined to set the world to rights, now has a new mission: to help her niece find her way back to happiness. Will Alyssa be reunited with Tom, or find a new love with Ruby's choice, handsome policeman Ben O'Hare?